I SWAPPED MY BROTHER ON THE INTERNET!

JO SIMMONS

Illustrated by **NATHAN REED**

BLOOMSBURY
LONDON OXFORD NEW YORK NEW DELHI SYDNEY

Bloomsbury Publishing, London, Oxford, New York, New Delhi and Sydney

First published in Great Britain in January 2018 by Bloomsbury Publishing Plc
50 Bedford Square, London WC1B 3DP

www.bloomsbury.com

BLOOMSBURY is a registered trademark of Bloomsbury Publishing Plc

A CIP catalogue record for this book is available from the British Library

ISBN 978 1 4088 7775 3

Printed and bound in Great Britain by CPI Group (UK) Ltd, Croydon CR0 4YY

1 3 5 7 9 10 8 6 4 2

For Paul, with love – I have never
wanted to swap you, not even after
the Dairylea triangle incident ...

CHAPTER ONE

CLICK!

CHANGE BROTHERS AND SWITCH SISTERS
TODAY WITH
www.siblingswap.com

The advert popped up in the corner of the screen. Jonny clicked on it instantly. The Sibling Swap website pinged open, showing smiling brothers and happy sisters, all playing and laughing and having a great time together.

What crazy alternative universe was this? Where were the big brothers teasing their little brothers about being rubbish at climbing and slow at everything? Where were the wedgies and ear flicks? What about the name-calling? This looked like a world

Jonny had never experienced, a world in which brothers and sisters actually *liked* each other!

'Oh sweet mangoes of heaven!' Jonny muttered.

It was pretty bonkers, but it was definitely tempting. No, scrap that: it was *essential*. Jonny couldn't believe his luck. Just think what Sibling Swap could offer him.

A new brother. A *better* brother. A brother who didn't put salt in his orange squash, who didn't call him a human sloth, who didn't burp in his ear. That kind of brother.

Jonny had to try it. He could always return the new brother if things didn't work out. It was a no-brainer.

He clicked on the application form.

What could go wrong?

CHAPTER TWO

FIGHT, FATE, FORMS

Only a little while before Jonny saw the Sibling Swap advert, he and his older brother, Ted, had had a fight. Another fight.

It was a particularly stupid fight, and it had started like all stupid fights do – over something stupid. This time, pants. But not just any pants. The Hanging Pants of Doom.

Jonny and Ted were walking their dog, Widget, on the nearby Common. They arrived at a patch of woodland, where an exceptionally large and colourful pair of men's pants had been hanging in a tree for ages. These pants had become legendary over the years the brothers had been playing here. There was a horrible glamour about them. The boys were grossed out and slightly scared of them, but could never quite ignore them. And so the pants had become the Hanging Pants of Doom, and now, unfortunately, Jonny had just lobbed Widget's Frisbee into the tree. It was stuck in a branch, just below the mythical underwear.

'Oh swear word,' said Jonny.

'Nice one!' said Ted. 'You threw it up there, so you have to get it down.'

Jonny frowned. Two problems presented themselves. One was the fact that the Frisbee was very close to the pants, making the possibility of touching the revolting garment very real. Second, Jonny wasn't very good at climbing.

'Go on, Jonny, up you go,' teased Ted. 'Widget can't wait all day for his Frisbee. Climb up and get it ... What's that? You're rubbish at climbing? Sorry, what? You would prefer it if I went and got the Frisbee, as I'm truly excellent at climbing?'

'All RIGHT!' fumed Jonny, ripping off his jacket. 'I'll climb up and get it. Look after my coat.'

'Thanks!' said Ted. 'I might use it as a blanket. You're so slow, we could be here until midnight.'

Jonny began his climb slowly, as Ted had predicted, and rather shakily, as Ted had also predicted.

'I'm just taking my time, going carefully. Don't rush me!' said Jonny, as he reached for the next branch.

'Spare us the running commentary,' Ted said.

After several minutes, a tiny dog appeared below the tree, followed by its elderly owner, and it began yapping up at Jonny.

'That's my brother up there,' Ted said to the

lady, pointing up. 'He's thrown his pants into the tree again and has to go and get them.'

The lady squinted up. Her dog continued yip-yapping.

'Oh yes, I see,' she said. 'Well, they're rather splendid pants, aren't they? I can see why he wants to get them back. Are those spaceships on them?'

'Cars,' said Ted.

'Very fetching,' said the lady. 'But he shouldn't throw them into the trees again. A magpie might get them.'

'That's what I told him,' said Ted, trying not to laugh. 'Sorry, I better go and help or we'll be here until Christmas. He's like a human sloth!'

With that, Ted bounced up into the tree, pulling himself quickly up its branches and passing his brother, just as Jonny was within touching distance of the Frisbee.

'Got it!' said Ted, snatching the Frisbee and tossing it down to Widget, before swinging off a branch and landing neatly on his feet. 'You can come down now, bro. Unless you really do want to touch the Pants of Doom. You're pretty close, actually. Look! They're just there.'

Jonny made a noise in his throat – a bit like a growl – and felt his face burning bright red. He was shaking with anger and humiliation as he slowly began making his way down.

By the time the brothers banged back into the house, Jonny was speechless with fury. He ran upstairs. He could hear his mum telling him off for slamming the front door, but too bad. He smashed his bedroom door shut too. There! How's that? He was sick of Ted teasing him, sick of being the younger brother. And as for telling that old lady that the Hanging Pants of Doom were *his* ...

Jonny flipped open his laptop and, miraculously, there was the Sibling Swap website telling him that all this could change. What perfect timing. Had the Sibling Swap team climbed into his head and read his thoughts? Who cared?

He read the home page:

SOMETIMES YOU DON'T GET THE BROTHER OR SISTER YOU DESERVE, BUT HERE AT SIBLING SWAP, WE AIM TO PUT THAT RIGHT. WITH SO MANY BROTHERS AND SISTERS OUT THERE, WE CAN MATCH YOU TO THE PERFECT ONE!

His heart began to beat faster.

SWAPPING YOUR BROTHER OR SISTER HAS NEVER BEEN EASIER WITH SIBLING SWAP! SIMPLY FILL OUT THE APPLICATION FORM

AND WE WILL SUPPLY YOU WITH A NEW BROTHER OR SISTER WITHIN TWENTY-FOUR HOURS, CAREFULLY CHOSEN FROM OUR MASSIVE DATABASE OF POSSIBLE MATCHES. OUR DEDICATED TEAM OF SWAP OPERATIVES WORKS 24/7 TO FIND THE BEST MATCH FOR YOU, BUT IF YOU ARE NOT COMPLETELY HAPPY, YOU CAN RETURN YOUR REPLACEMENT SIBLING FOR A NEW MATCH OR YOUR ORIGINAL BROTHER OR SISTER.

Amazing! For the first time in his almost ten years, this website was offering Jonny power, choice, freedom! It felt good! He rubbed his hands together and began filling out the form.

First, there were two options:

ARE YOU SWAPPING A SIBLING?

ARE YOU PUTTING YOURSELF UP TO BE SWAPPED?

'Easy,' Jonny muttered. 'I'm the one doing the swapping. Me. I have the power!' He did a sort of evil genius laugh as he clicked on the top box. By Tic Tacs, this was exciting! Next, the form asked:

ARE YOU SWAPPING A BROTHER OR SISTER?

'Also easy,' muttered Jonny. 'Brother.'
Then:

WOULD YOU LIKE TO RECEIVE A BROTHER OR A SISTER?

Jonny clicked the box marked 'Brother'. Then he had to add some information about himself.

AGE: NINE.
HOBBIES: BIKING, SWIMMING, COMPUTER GAMES, DOUGHNUTS, MESSING ABOUT.
LEAST FAVOURITE THINGS:
- **MY BROTHER, TED (HE TEASES ME ALL**

THE TIME AND RECKONS HE'S COOL JUST BECAUSE HE GOES TO SECONDARY SCHOOL)

- **BEING NINE (I *AM* NEARLY TEN, BUT CAN I HAVE A BROTHER WHO IS YOUNGER THAN ME OR MAYBE THE SAME AGE PLEASE?)**
- **SPROUTS**
- **CLIMBING**
- **BEING SICK**

Then there was a whole page about the kind of brother Jonny might like. He quickly ticked the following boxes: fun; adventurous; enjoys food; enjoys sports and swimming; likes dogs. He didn't tick the box marked 'living' or the one marked 'human'. He just wanted a brother, so it was obvious, wasn't it?

That ought to do it, Jonny reckoned. His heart was galloping now. In just three minutes it was ready to send. He sat back in his chair. 'Just one click,' he said, 'and I get a brother upgrade by this time tomorrow. Friday, in fact! Ready for the weekend!'

Jonny felt slightly dizzy. He giggled quietly to himself. He felt giddy with power! All he had to do was send off the form. Easy! But then he hesitated ... Should he do this? Was it OK? Would he get into trouble? Jonny's dad no longer lived with him and Ted, so he might not notice, but what would his mum say? She'd be pleased, Jonny decided quickly. Yes! After all, she was fed up with Jonny and Ted arguing. This was the perfect solution. Then, with a tiny frown, he wondered how Ted might feel about being swapped, but before he could puzzle this out, there was his brother again, shouting up the stairs.

'Dinner, loser!' Ted yelled. 'Let me know if you need help climbing down the stairs.

They *are* quite steep. It could take you a while.'

That was it! For the second time that day, Jonny felt the anger bubbling up inside like a can of shaken Pixie Fizz. Enough! Double enough!

'So I'm the rubbish younger brother, am I? Well, here's one thing I can do really brilliantly,' he muttered and, jutting out his chin, hit the send button.

CLICK!

'Done!' he said, and slammed the laptop shut.

CHAPTER THREE

GONE

Jonny had a strange dream that night. The doorbell rang, and when he answered it there was a new brother on the doorstep. Only it wasn't a boy, it was a tiny squirrel wearing a green suit, eating a cheese sandwich.

Jonny woke with a start, sat up and rubbed his eyes. Then he remembered! He'd done it! He had swapped Ted, and today, hopefully, his new, improved extra-much-better-er brother would arrive.

'You look excited,' his best friend, George, said at school later. Jonny was tapping his pen feverishly on his desk. 'Like, massively excited. What's going on?'

'Just a bit of family improvement,' said Jonny. Then he leaned across so he was really close to George. 'You won't believe this, but I've swapped Ted!' he whispered.

'Swapped him?' asked George.

'Yes! I'm getting a new brother today. Cool, eh?'

'How? On a website?'

'Yes, have you heard of it? There's this Sibling Swap site where they match you up with a new brother or sister. I had to try it! He's arriving after school.'

George stared hard at Jonny, his eyebrows raised, and was about to speak when their teacher, Mrs Flannery, told the boys to stop whispering and concentrate on their spellings.

As soon as the final bell rang, Jonny raced home. His hand trembled with excitement as he put his key in the door. Once inside, he stood still and listened.

'Ted?' he called out. 'You there?'

Silence.

Jonny looked in the living room.

'No Ted in here,' he whispered. 'I'm talking to myself, but never mind.'

He moved down the corridor. 'No Ted in the kitchen! So far, so good!'

Then he bounded upstairs.

'Bathroom?' he said, looking in. 'Ted-free! My bedroom? Yup, also no sign of an older brother.'

Finally, Jonny paused outside Ted's room. His lair, big brother headquarters, the inner sanctum. A sign on the door said BABY BROTHERS KEEP OUT. With a gulp, Jonny ignored it and stepped cautiously into the room.

Empty.

He sat down on Ted's bed and glanced around. He grinned and then put his hand over his mouth like he'd said a rude word. Then he began to bounce, just a little. Then a little more. Then he leaped up on to the bed, shoes on and everything, and jumped up and down wildly, slapping the ceiling and whooping with glee. Finally, he crashed back on to the bed, panting.

'There doesn't seem to be a single Ted in the house,' he said. 'Now, why is that, I wonder? Ooh, hang on, wait a minute. Is it because Ted was so annoying that his brother decided to swap him on the internet? Yes, I think so. And is that same brother now waiting for a Ted replacement to arrive? Yes, that's right!'

BING BONG.

The doorbell rang.

'And here he is!' said Jonny. 'Let the fun brother times begin!'

CHAPTER FOUR

MEET MERVYN

Jonny sped down the stairs and yanked the front door open. Standing on the mat was a small boy, roughly the same age as Jonny, with blond hair and a big smile.

'Hello,' said Jonny.

'Hello,' said the boy.

'Are you ... ?' said Jonny.

'That's right!' said the boy.

'Come to be my new ...'

'Yes!' said the boy.

'Great!' said Jonny.

'I know!' said the boy. 'I'm really ...'

'Me too!'

Both boys were grinning now, like their faces had been stretched. Widget sat between them, looking from one to the other.

'He's nice,' said the boy, pointing at Widget. 'Doesn't talk much, does he?'

'Talk much? No, s'pose not. He can bark, though, can't he?'

'Can he? Of course,' said the boy. 'Can I come in?'

'Oh crumbs, sorry, yes,' said Jonny. 'Hang on! What's your name?'

'Mervyn,' said the boy.

'Cool name!' said Jonny. 'Welcome, Mervyn. I'm Jonny. This is Widget. Let's have some milk to celebrate.'

Mervyn followed Jonny into the kitchen. He couldn't stop smiling. He had actually got himself a new brother and, so far, the new brother was great. Nice blond hair. A big smile. Slightly odd clothes, like he'd borrowed them from someone who was cool three decades ago, but whatever. The main thing was that Mervyn was pleased to see Jonny, which was refreshing. Ted was never pleased to see Jonny.

'So what do you like to do?' Jonny asked. 'I love riding bikes and swimming. Probably those are my best things.'

'Me too!' said Mervyn. 'Well, swimming, anyway. I've never tried riding a bike.'

Jonny spat out his milk in surprise. 'Never ridden a bike?' he spluttered.

'No,' said Mervyn.

'Not even once?'

'Well, we, er, just don't go in for bikes where I'm from.'

'Where *are* you from? Bonkersville? A weird alternate universe where there are no bikes at all anywhere?'

'Erm … kind of. You're close,' said Mervyn.

'You're not from outer space, are you?' Jonny asked, grinning.

'No!' said Mervyn, giggling. 'That would be silly!'

'Yes, that would be silly,' agreed Jonny and the two boys laughed.

'It's fine, anyway,' Jonny continued, thinking. 'My mum's Auntie Bee has never learned to drive a car and she's sixty-two, *and* she's never had a Jaffa Cake. I offered her one once but she wouldn't even try it.'

'What's a Jaffa Cake?' Mervyn asked.

Jonny stared at him for a split second, but decided to move on. He'd had an idea.

'I know!' he said. 'I can teach you to ride a bike.'

'Really?' said Mervyn. 'Would you do that for me?'

'Absolutely, brother!' said Jonny. 'That's what brothers do for each other. Well, nice brothers anyway. And I'm definitely a nice one, promise! Come on, let's try right now!'

CHAPTER FIVE

ON YOUR BIKE!

Jonny pulled his bike out from the side of the house and wheeled it over to Mervyn, who stood waiting on the pavement.

'You can have my bike,' said Jonny. 'I'll use Ted's. I'm the big brother now, after all.'

He went back for Ted's bike. Now that he was standing next to it, it was obvious the

bike was too big for him. But he wasn't going
to be put off.

'Look and learn, Merv. You sit here,
put your feet on the pedals and just push
off …'

Jonny hopped on to Ted's bike, wobbled a
bit and began cruising down the pavement.
Only then did he realise that his feet could
barely reach the pedals.

'Are you meant to wobble like that?' Mervyn
called. 'Wow, you're going very fast, Jonny!

I like that shouty noise you're making! Watch out for that creature in the way! Is it a seal? Mind the big green thing ... Oh help, you crashed right into it. Is that fun, or ... ? It looks slightly painful. Are you meant to do that? Hang on, you're stuck ...'

The creature Jonny had swerved to avoid was not a seal. It was Stanley. Or Fat Stanley, as Jonny and Ted called him. He was the overweight cat belonging to their neighbour, Mrs Algernon. By avoiding Stanley, Jonny had crashed straight into her hedge.

This was not good. Firstly, because Mrs Algernon took pride in the neatness of her hedge, but also because she was known for being grim and serious, so the chances of her finding Jonny's crash at all funny were basically zero. Jonny had never seen her smile – ever! It was like she didn't believe in smiling. By the time Mervyn caught up with him, Mrs Algernon had come out of her house. She looked properly miffed. Of course …

'You've dented my privet,' she said.

Jonny's head and shoulders were still trapped in the hedge. Mervyn helped pull him out. Jonny fell backwards on to the pavement and tugged a handful of twigs out of his hair. 'Sorry!' he said, when he saw Mrs Algernon glowering.

'Are you all right?' Mervyn asked.

'Think so,' said Jonny. 'I meant to do that. Absolutely! All part of the plan, you know?'

Mervyn looked confused.

'All right, so the falling into the hedge bit wasn't quite what I meant to do,' said Jonny. He brushed some leaves off his sleeve.

'It wasn't completely my fault! I mean, the bike is way bigger than I realised, and then Stanley was there and I had to swerve to avoid him, and then the hedge was there and

I had to …' Jonny petered out. 'OK, it was a disaster!'

Mervyn began to laugh. Then Jonny laughed too. Then both boys glanced at Mrs Algernon, whose face looked stern enough to split boulders. And that was it. The two boys collapsed into uncontrollable giggles while Mrs Algernon continued to glare at them, arms folded across her considerable bosom. Finally, Jonny pulled himself together.

'Lucky your hedge was there,' he said to Mrs Algernon. Her expression suggested she didn't agree. 'I'm teaching him to ride a bike,' he added, pointing at Mervyn.

Mrs Algernon raised her eyebrows. 'If you so much as look at my hedge again, let alone touch it, land in it, dent it or damage it in any way whatsoever, you will feel the full force of my fury,' she said.

'Sure thing, Mrs A,' said Jonny, saluting and then wincing.

'Are you hurt?' Mervyn asked.

'I'll be fine, but thanks for asking. Ted, my old brother, would have really taken the mickey out of me if he'd just seen me fall into a hedge.'

'Well, I'm not Ted,' said Mervyn.

'No,' said Jonny, smiling. 'You're really not!'

CHAPTER SIX

FISHY BUSINESS

When the boys got home, Jonny's mum was in the kitchen, laying the table.

'It's fish fingers for dinner,' she said. 'Your friend's welcome to stay, Jonny.'

'This is Mervyn,' said Jonny, but his mum didn't hear. She was searching for the ketchup, her head deep inside a kitchen cupboard.

'Fish fingers again,' said Jonny. 'I should have guessed. My friend George has this uncle who's always trying new schemes to make money and whatnot, and the last thing he was doing was selling fish fingers. Only he couldn't. Sell them all, that is, so he's gone on to some other new business idea, I suppose, and George has given us boxes and boxes of the fish fingers he doesn't want. Hey, are you OK?'

Mervyn was drooling.

'Yes, sorry,' he said, wiping the dribble on his sleeve.

Mervyn ate greedily at dinner, picking up the fish fingers in his hands and devouring them. He chomped noisily too, his mouth open, the fish fingers tumbling around it like pants in a washing machine.

'I must tell George how much you're enjoying his uncle's fish fingers,' said Jonny, as Mervyn stuffed one after another into his mouth. 'Personally, I'm a bit over them, but ...'

Mervyn kept on chomping.

'Why don't you have some chips too?' said Jonny as Mervyn grabbed another fish finger. 'Chips are the food of the angels. Or some ketchup? I call this magic sauce, because it makes everything taste good.'

Mervyn didn't respond. He was too busy guzzling.

'Leave some room, Merv,' said Jonny. 'There's ice cream for pudding.'

Mervyn just shook his head and carried on chomping.

'We should probably keep a few back for Jonny's brother, Ted,' said Jonny's mum. 'He'll be home soon.'

'He's at Jim's house,' Jonny said quickly. 'Staying the whole weekend, I think.'

'Is he?'

'Yes,' said Jonny. 'Remember?'

'Do I remember?' said his mum, giving it some thought. 'No, I don't. But I'm sure you're right, Jonny. I'd forget my head if it wasn't screwed on! I think I'm getting worse. At remembering. Am I getting worse?'

'No, Mum, you're perfect,' he said, but inside he was doing a huge *Phew!* Thank heavens his mum was a bit vague sometimes. It meant she believed Ted was away for the weekend. The coast was clear! The weekend was here. Jonny now had lots of free time to get to know his new brother.

'Maybe we could go swimming tomorrow?' Jonny suggested.

'Ooh yes!' Mervyn said. 'But actually, no, perhaps not, I'm not sure about that.'

'Why not? You love swimming. You said.'

'I've got a bit of a cold,' said Mervyn.

'You seem fine.'

'Tummy ache, I mean.'

'Probably because you just ate three hundred and sixty-two fish fingers,' said Jonny.

'I might go and have a bath,' said Mervyn.

'Really? Wouldn't you prefer another bike lesson? Or a go on the Xbox?'

But Mervyn was already on his way

upstairs. Seconds later Jonny heard the lock on the bathroom door click.

Jonny wasn't a huge fan of baths. Mervyn, though, seemed to really love having a bath, because he was in there for ages. Take the amount of time a bath-lover might spend in the tub, and then add on another half an hour. At least.

'Are you all right?' Jonny asked eventually, banging on the bathroom door. 'You've been in there for about six years. You haven't drowned, have you?'

Mervyn made a strange squeaky sound. Had he sat on a guinea pig? Was he in pain? Then Jonny heard splashing. Loud, major splashing.

'Mervyn?' he said. 'That's a lot of splashing. What's going on?'

More really splashy splashing.

'Are you all right?' Jonny shouted through

the door. 'Did you get your toe stuck in the tap? Have you licked the soap? Are you choking on a flannel? Is someone else in there? Are you being attacked? Oh no! Mrs Algernon! And the full force of her fury! Did she climb up the drainpipe? It's revenge for the hedge squashing, isn't it? You're being attacked and it's all my fault!'

Jonny felt desperate. He tried the door. Locked! He rattled it. The splashing got louder. He began to feel real panic. He rattled some more.

'I'm coming, brother!' he yelled, frantically joggling the door handle. 'I'll save you! I'll ...'

CRASH!

The lock gave way, the door flew open and Jonny rushed into the room, slipped on the splashed water and landed on his back on the floor.

'Oof!' he said.

Slowly, he sat up and looked around. The room was empty. No Mrs Algernon in ninja gear, her tiny eyes blazing with rage as she attempted to strangle his new brother.

'There's no one here!' he said.

Only Mervyn, of course, peeping at Jonny from one end of the bath. And at the other end? Not Mervyn's feet and toes but an enormous, scaly, silver fishtail flapping against the taps.

'What's that?' cried Jonny, staring at the huge tail.

He stood up shakily. Now he could see all of Mervyn. Only not all of Mervyn looked like Mervyn. The lower half of Mervyn, where his legs used to be, had turned into a fish's enormous tail. Mervyn grabbed a flannel and tried to cover it.

'Don't hate me! I know it's a bit weird,' said Mervyn.

'Oh, that is so ...'

Mervyn flinched. 'Odd? Strange? Yes, I
know, but I can explain! I –'

'COOL!' said Jonny, his eyes lighting up.
'That is so cool! Solid gold cool! You are a
mermaid!'

Jonny gawped at him, his eyes wide with
wonder. Mervyn cleared his throat.

'*Boy*, actually,' he said.

'Sorry, yes,' said Jonny, slapping his forehead in an 'I'm so stupid' way. 'A *boymaid*!'

'No, I'm a *merboy*!' said Mervyn. *'Mer* followed by *boy*!'

'Merboy, merboy, merboy,' muttered Jonny, still trying to take it all in. 'Absolutely! Of course. I mean, not of course, actually. This is not at *all* normal, you know. It's not every day your new brother turns into a fish in the bath. I mean a merboy.'

'Are you angry?' Mervyn asked.

'What? No!' said Jonny. 'Are you kidding? This is one hundred per cent awesome! But how can you get your legs back?'

'I just need to dry off,' said Mervyn. He didn't move, and neither did Jonny.

'In private?' said Mervyn.

'Oh, of course, sure!' said Jonny, still staring at his new brother's fishy lower half. 'It's just so incredible! Your tail! You've got a tail. And scales. Oh, too good! Anyway, meet me back downstairs when you've de-merboy-ed yourself. Amazing! Just amazing!'

CHAPTER SEVEN

SECRET SWIMMING PLANS

When Mervyn walked back into the kitchen, Jonny burst out laughing.

'Look at you walking!' he said. 'When a minute ago you had a ...'

'Shhh!' said Mervyn. 'I think we should keep this quiet. I don't want to attract attention. I've only just arrived on land!'

'Is that why you've never ridden a bike?' Jonny asked. 'Bikes don't work in the sea!'

Mervyn nodded.

'And is that why you didn't want to go swimming?'

'Yes, as soon as my legs get properly wet, I turn into a merboy,' Mervyn said. 'Feels weird, though, this whole walking about on legs thing. I'm used to swimming everywhere.'

'Well, let's go swimming!' said Jonny. 'We must be able to find water somewhere. The leisure centre is out – too public ...'

'Could we go to the sea?' Mervyn asked. 'I'd love to see it again. It's the only home I've ever known. My parents put me on Sibling Swap because they wanted me to try life on dry land. They kept going on about all the opportunities up here. It's great here, isn't it? Houses and bikes and you, of course, my new brother. I know I'll get used to it, it's just all so different to the sea ...'

'It takes a while to get to the beach in the car,' said Jonny. 'And I can't drive. I'm too young. Maybe tomorrow? I could ask my mum. Perhaps we could try the pond on the Common for now. It's a bit brown, usually with a few plastic bottles floating in it. Plus, the ducks might give you a funny look.'

'How deep is it?' Mervyn asked.

'Pretty deep. There's a sign next to it saying DEEP WATER, so it's deep enough for a DEEP WATER sign.'

'Great!' said Mervyn. 'When can we go?'

Jonny looked out of the window and then at the clock.

'In about an hour, when the light starts to fade and there's nobody about,' he said. 'The perfect time for some outdoor, not-strictly-allowed-but-never-mind merboy swimming fun! Whoop!'

CHAPTER EIGHT

POND DIPPING

An hour later Mervyn and Jonny left the house and snuck off down the street.

Jonny felt fizzed-up with eagerness. This was the life, eh? Off out at dusk, eh? With your brother, eh? To have adventures and scrapes and fun and more adventures, eh?

Soon the two boys were standing at the edge of the pond.

'What do you reckon?' Jonny asked.

'It'll do,' said Mervyn, and he ripped off his corduroy flares and dived straight in, disappearing under the water.

Jonny watched to see where he would surface.

Nothing.

'He'll pop up in a minute,' he said to himself, scanning the pond.

Nothing. Silence.

'Come on, Mervyn, up you come,' Jonny muttered, beginning to feel uneasy. 'Give me a wave.'

Still nothing. By now the water was perfectly still. Jonny started to feel anxious.

'Mervyn!' he yelled. 'Where are you?'

He needs to come up to breathe, Jonny thought. *He's like a whale, isn't he, or a dolphin? He needs to pop up and get some air. So where is he? Is he all right? Has he got tangled in a shopping trolley or attacked by killer crayfish?*

Jonny hopped about by the pond for a few seconds and then remembered how Ted always teased him for being slow. *Right,* he thought. *I can't wait. I have to help Mervyn. He's in a weird brown pond instead of the nice big sea, and he's my brother. Time to act!*

'Hang on, Mervyn!' Jonny yelled, pulling off his trainers. 'I'm going to find you!'

He waded into the water. His feet squelched on the squelchy stuff at the bottom of the pond. He hoped it was mud but guessed it was probably duck poo. Never mind!

He had to save his new brother. The water was up to his thighs now but Jonny hardly noticed, he was too busy looking for any sign of Mervyn in the dim light. He called out to him, squinted through the dusk, then ...

'QUACK!'

A duck flew out of nowhere, right under Jonny's nose.

He jumped in fright, slipped and plunged face first into the middle of the pond. The murky water closed over his head. He couldn't see. His feet skated on the bottom, his hands grasped at slippery weeds. *Help me!* he thought.

Then, suddenly, he had the sensation of being pulled along. He opened his eyes for a second, saw a flash of silvery fishtail and then burst up to the surface like a cork out of a bottle.

Mervyn was by his side, holding him up. 'Did you fancy a swim too?' he joked.

'You didn't come up for air,' Jonny spluttered as he scrambled back to dry land. 'I thought you'd drowned.'

'I can breathe under water,' said Mervyn. 'All merpeople can.'

'Well, that's just mer-vellous, isn't it,' said Jonny, crashing on to the bank like a drunken starfish.

CHAPTER NINE

SPLASH!

While Jonny towelled himself off, Mervyn gave a merboyish squeak and swam around the pond again. Jonny could just make out his beautiful tail glinting in the dying light of the day. It was an impressive sight. He looked so happy and natural in the water. Jonny didn't want to stop his fun, but he was beginning to shiver, so he shouted to him to come out.

As Mervyn pulled himself on to the bank; his tail shimmered in the moonlight.

Jonny passed him the towel and turned away while Mervyn rubbed his tail. Then, with a 'Ta da!', he flicked Jonny with the towel. There were his legs again.

'Does that mean we can walk home

now?' said Jonny, pointing at Mervyn's lower half.

Mervyn laughed, and the two boys set off.

As Jonny squelched on to the doorstep, Mervyn laid a hand on his arm.

'Thanks for that,' he said. 'I know you got wet, but thanks. It felt so good to be swimming again.'

Tucked up in bed that night, Jonny decided that Friday with his new brother Mervyn had been good. A bit wet, a bit hedge-y, but exciting and different and good. He drifted off, lulled by the sound of rain beginning to fall outside.

It was still tipping it down outside in the morning, so the boys watched TV. There was a nature programme on, about the oceans. Mervyn chatted all the way through it.

'Seals are real show-offs,' he said. 'Look at that one! Hang on! I know him. That's Sammy! Hey, Sammy, how are you? Good moves! Ah, he's a lovely guy. Terrible fishy breath, but he's a brilliant swimmer. Ooh, look, here come the killer whales. Look out, everybody! You have to watch out for them. They hang out in big gangs and they're very slippery, in a can't-trust-them way. And literally, too, I suppose. I've never touched one, so I don't know. But someone told me once that they calm down if you tickle their dorsal fin. That's a good tip for you!'

'Spare us the running commentary,' Jonny murmured, then frowned as he realised this was something Ted used to say to him.

Jonny chased this thought away by looking out of the window.

'The rain's stopped,' he said. 'Let's go to the park.'

Mervyn sniffed the air as he stepped outside.

'I can smell the water everywhere,' he said.

Jonny had no idea that water had a smell, but it certainly was wet out. It had rained for hours. The leaves on the trees were dripping fat droplets that ran down the back of your neck and made you shudder. Water rushed along the road, and the cars made a whooshing sound as they ploughed through it.

Mervyn hesitated.

'Worried about all this water setting you off?' Jonny asked. 'Don't be! I'll keep an eye out for any extra-large puddles.'

As the boys passed the doctor's surgery at the end of Jonny's road, Mervyn caught sight of the fish tank in the waiting room. He stood for a while, gazing at it through the window. Jonny watched too. Which was why neither of them spotted the truck until it was too late. The truck that was travelling up the road, towards a huge pool that had formed around a blocked drain.

'Come on, fish fan, let's go,' Jonny said, and as the two boys turned, Jonny saw it ...

The fat tyres were about to rip through the brown pool of water and splat it straight over them. It would be a total drench-out.

'Nooo!' shouted Jonny, throwing his arms wide, trying to create a human shield between Mervyn and the water that was leaping up from the truck's wheels in a huge wet arc.

The water seemed to move in slow motion. It crashed into Jonny first, then splatted down on Mervyn behind him.

Jonny wiped the water from his eyes and turned. Where was Mervyn?

'Down here!' Mervyn said in a squeaky whisper.

He was lying on the pavement, flapping like a fish out of water, in full merboy mode. 'Cover my tail, quick, before anybody sees!'

Jonny ripped off his top and flung it over Mervyn, but it didn't cover the tail completely. The pointy end was still in plain sight. Quickly, Jonny lay across it.

'What are you doing?' Mervyn asked.

'Hiding your tail and drying it with my body!'

While Jonny squashed and warmed the tail, Mervyn began rubbing at its sides with the top.

'Come on, come on!' Mervyn muttered, as his legs refused to reappear.

Suddenly, Jonny felt a pain in his back. He turned to see an old man, who had just come out of the doctor's surgery. He had a wooden walking stick, which he was using to prod Jonny.

'What are you two up to?' the man asked. 'Fighting?'

'No, we're, we're – what are we doing? We're

dancing!' shouted Jonny (it was all he could come up with in the heat of the moment).

'Funny sort of dance,' said the man. 'You're right in the way. I could have tripped over you! Clear off!'

'No thanks!' said Jonny. 'We're having too much fun. Besides, we're in the finals of the national pavement sitting-down dancing competition next week. We need to practise.'

'Go and practise somewhere else,' said the old man, and muttered something about how this wouldn't have happened in his day.

Jonny didn't get up straight away. He didn't dare! He couldn't tell whether Mervyn's legs had returned. The old man prodded Jonny with his stick again, but Jonny refused to budge. Ted often accused him of being slow, but right now Jonny was in no rush to reveal that his new brother was a merboy. He had to stall the man …

'Could you just step over us?' Jonny asked.

'With *my* knees?' huffed the old man. 'You must be batty! Now come on, clear the path!'

Slowly and carefully, but mostly just slowly, Jonny stood up.

'About time,' said the old man. Not 'Wow, a mermaid!' or 'Help! Police! A fish-kid lying on the pavement!' Thank cheeses! Mervyn's legs were back.

'That was close!' said Jonny.

'A bit too close!' said Mervyn, standing up unsteadily. 'Can we go home now?'

CHAPTER TEN

THE SEA, THE SEA

Mervyn was quiet when the boys got home. Jonny felt sorry for him. Having to worry that his legs were going to turn into a fish-tail every time he went out, causing mass panic and major embarrassment, must be hard. But in among all this, Jonny also felt a tiny bit worried for himself too. What if Mervyn went full merboy again? And again? Jonny wasn't sure he could think up enough clever excuses for why he was lying on top of his brother. The pavement-dancing competition was genius, but what if he couldn't come up with something as good next time?

These were difficult thoughts, and Jonny wasn't a fan of difficult thoughts. He preferred thoughts about doughnuts, pugs that wore

Superman costumes, or being able to do magic. So, to chase the difficult thoughts away, Jonny suggested a trip to the seaside. Perhaps being near the sea would perk Mervyn up a bit?

His mum agreed to take them. Mervyn looked pleased, Jonny felt excited and Widget the dog ... Well, he had no idea where he was going, but he hopped enthusiastically into the back seat of the car and sat between the two boys.

The clouds had blown away by the time they arrived at the seaside, and the boys ran happily on to the sand, with Widget barking and leaping between them. Jonny and Mervyn built a castle with a deep moat, and then went to look for shells to decorate it.

'The sea is so beautiful, isn't it?' said Mervyn, staring at it like he was in a dream.

'S'pose so,' said Jonny. 'Nice and big and wet.'

Mervyn started making those strange squeaking sounds Jonny had heard him make in the bath. Like a dolphin crossed with a piglet.

Jonny threw a pebble into the sea and Widget bounded in after it. Then, suddenly, there was another huge splash. Mervyn had plunged in too.

'It's all right,' Jonny called. 'Widget can swim!'

But Mervyn wasn't rescuing the dog. Mervyn was off!

Jonny stared out to sea. Finally, he saw a head surface a long way out and a tiny arm waving. Then, nothing.

'He's *gone!*' said Jonny, half upset, half outraged. How could he swim off like that?

Then he noticed Mervyn's corduroy trousers on the sand. He picked them up. There was a note sticking out of one pocket.

Dear Jonny,

If you are reading this, it's because I have decided to rip off my trousers, jump into the waves and go away to sea. Sorry. I will miss you. You were a great brother. You were kind. You tried to protect me from the spray this morning and even went into a pond to rescue me (which was a tiny bit stupid but kind of mervellous!). So, thanks loads. I won't forget you. If I can help you in the future, just call my name! (By the way, I may not hear you because the sea is very big, but feel free to try …)

Mervyn

Jonny tucked the note into his pocket and walked back to his mum.

'Where's your friend?' she asked.

'He had to go home,' said Jonny.

'Shame,' she said. 'He seemed nice.'

He was nice, thought Jonny, feeling a bit sad. But he understood. The call of the sea was too strong for Mervyn. He had to live there. It wasn't fair for a merboy to live on land. It wasn't natural. It would be like asking Jonny to live up a tree or underground or in Hemel Hempstead. All wrong!

Then Jonny remembered Sibling Swap and suddenly glowed with excitement. Mervyn may have gone, but there were lots more brothers where he came from. Well, not *exactly* where he came from. Jonny didn't want another merboy, but what were the chances of that happening? Zero! No, for sure, the next brother would be happiest on land and – Jonny could feel it – absolutely perfect.

CHAPTER ELEVEN

SECOND TIME LUCKY?

Jonny emailed the Sibling Swap offices when he got home to tell them that Mervyn had gone away to sea and to ask for a new brother. He soon got an email back from one of the Swap operatives.

'Good news, Swapper! We have a perfect match for you. We're sure this Swap won't flop! He will arrive at 6 p.m.'

'Six p.m.?' said Jonny. 'That's two hours away. I better get ready!'

Then he realised that he didn't really know what getting ready involved, so he went and had a little nap instead. His best friend, George, popped in after that, and the two boys drank some milk together in the kitchen.

'How's the new brother going?' George

asked, looking a tiny bit anxious. 'Has he arrived yet?'

'Been and gone, I'm afraid,' said Jonny. 'Loved your uncle's fish fingers, though. Ate millions of them!'

'Good!' said George. 'I'm sure I can get you some more. He's still got a massive load of them at his warehouse. I'm using it now for one of my projects, and there are freezers stuffed with fish fingers there.'

'Nah, you're OK,' said Jonny. 'I'm over fish fingers. Ooh, is that the time? You'd better go, George. I've requested another brother from Sibling Swap. He'll be here soon.'

'Can I meet him?' George asked.

'Soon,' said Jonny, ushering George out of the kitchen and opening the front door. 'Once he's settled in.'

'OK, but let me know how it's going, won't you?' said George.

'Yeah, yeah, sure,' said Jonny. 'Bye!'

Then 6 p.m. arrived. The doorbell rang, but when Jonny opened the door there was nobody there. Well, nobody on the front step, anyway. There was, however, a tall, skinny boy with small dark eyes standing on Jonny's garden wall, looking eagerly up and down the street. His arms were hanging down in front of his body, his fingers pointing neatly towards the ground, and his nose was twitching busily.

'Hello? Were you sent by Sibling Swap?' Jonny asked the boy.

The boy just squeaked and then half ran, half pounced into the house.

Different, thought Jonny. *But different can be good!*

He found the boy in the kitchen, standing on a chair, staring out of the window.

'Not much of a view, I'm afraid,' said Jonny.

'Just the back of the houses on the next street. What's your name?'

The boy squeaked again, jumped down and showed Jonny a tag which was hanging around his neck.

It said, simply, HARI.

'Hari,' said Jonny, pronouncing it 'Harry'.

Squeak squeak. The boy looked irritated.

'Hah-reee?' Jonny tried again.

The boy squeaked, then ran happily around the room on all fours.

'Nice one!' Jonny said, watching him. 'I did put on my form that I like messing about, after all, so you're bang on there. Can I join you? What are we pretending to be? Badgers? I do a great badger impression. Ted hates it! You'd never catch him leaping about like this in full animal mode. Wow, you're good, but check this out!'

Jonny sprung down on all fours and the

two boys scampered about for a while, until Jonny sat down on the floor, puffing.

'Do you want a drink, Hari?' he asked the boy, who so far had said nothing. But Hari didn't seem to be listening. He'd spotted a daddy-long-legs butting itself pointlessly against the ceiling. Quick as a flash he pounced, caught it in his mouth and began munching. One long insect leg poked out.

It seemed to be waving at Jonny. *This is taking pretending to be an animal a bit far*, he thought. It was straying into flat-out weird territory.

'What *are* you?' Jonny asked, staring. Hari rubbed his cheeks with his hands, like a creature cleaning its whiskers, then came and stood next to Jonny. He stood really close and really straight, huddling against his new brother.

'Are you a human cat?' Jonny asked. 'A weasel kid? A badger boy?'

Hari wouldn't look at him. He just stood there, pressed against him, surveying the room. Then Jonny had an idea. He ran upstairs and grabbed his encyclopaedia of animals from his bookcase. Back in the kitchen, he began flicking through it.

'Dugongs and manatees, no; great cats, no; lemurs, no,' said Jonny, flicking quickly.

'Hang on, maybe you are a lemur, or, I mean, pretending to be one?'

He showed a picture to Hari, who squeaked twice.

'What does that mean? No or yes?'

Hari began scratching his ear with his foot.

'Let's test this out. We need to find a way to speak,' said Jonny. 'Hari! Your name is Hari, right?'

Hari squeaked a single squeak.

'So one squeak is yes, and two is no,' said Jonny. 'Are you a lemur?'

Hari squeaked twice.

'Fine. Not a lemur,' said Jonny, continuing to flick through the pages. 'Elephant shrew?'

Two squeaks.

'European hamster?'

Two squeaks.

'Crested porcupine? Grey climbing mouse? Botta's pocket gopher?'

Two more squeaks, then Hari grabbed the book, flicked through it rapidly and passed it back to Jonny.

'Meerkat!' shrieked Jonny. 'Of course! All that standing up straight. It says here, ummm, yes, here we go: "One animal in the group stands on guard as sentinel." That's you! You're on guard, aren't you?'

One squeak.

'I get it!' said Jonny. 'Or do I?'

CHAPTER TWELVE

RAISED BY . . .

Jonny gazed at Hari for a while, thinking.

'OK, I'll admit it, I'm not sure I do get it,' he said. 'I mean, sorry to mention this and please don't take this the wrong way, but you're not *actually* a meerkat, are you?'

Hari blinked.

'You act like a meerkat, sure, but I don't see any fur, and you are kind of big for one,' Jonny went on.

Hari pointed at the picture of a family of meerkats. Then he ran over to the bookshelf where some photos were lined up. Hari pointed at a photo of Jonny's mum and then at the adult meerkat in the book.

'That's your mum?' said Jonny, trying not to make a 'you're frying my brains right now' face.

'*Squeak!*'

'Were you somehow, maybe, possibly, kind of *raised* by meerkats?' Jonny asked.

Another single squeak from Hari, who then rolled on his back happily before hopping up on to the chair and staring out of the window.

Jonny tried to take all this in. He had wanted a new brother, it's true. Someone quite different to Ted, yes. But there was 'quite different' and then there was 'a boy who thinks he is a meerkat different.' Yes, it would be pretty mad and exciting to have a boy who was raised by meerkats for a brother, but Jonny couldn't help thinking that this wasn't *really* what he'd signed up for. And before he realised he was speaking aloud, he was speaking aloud.

'This wasn't really what I signed up for,' he said.

Hari didn't reply. Something had caught his eye outside. The sandpit!

Leaping off the chair, he opened the back door and zoomed out into the garden. Jonny hadn't played in the sandpit for about a year, and it was full of leaves and, quite possibly, fox poops, but Hari didn't seem to care. He started excavating with his two hands, spraying sand out through his legs. He was trying to build a tunnel, but every time he climbed down it, it collapsed. He was too big!

Jonny guessed that this must have happened back home, wherever Hari came from – meerkat world. He'd got too big for the underground meerkat houses and so here he was, attempting to live in a regular human home.

Jonny joined Hari in the garden and, with a spade, tried to make the tunnel bigger, but there just wasn't enough sand and they both gave up after a while.

'Are you hungry after all that digging?' Jonny asked him. He ran back into the kitchen and brought Hari some bread, but Hari wasn't interested.

'You have to eat,' said Jonny, feeling concerned. 'All right, I know, let's go on a bug hunt.'

The two boys poked about in the bushes for a bit. Hari nibbled a worm and Jonny caught another daddy-long-legs and passed it to him. He looked away as Hari gobbled it down.

Quietly, Jonny sat back in the sandpit and built a little castle. Though Hari would probably never do something like that, he definitely needed sand – and lots more than Jonny had – so he could build the tunnel of his dreams. Perhaps it wouldn't be right for Hari living here. He needed a brother in the desert perhaps. Or one who lived right next to a beach … Jonny went back inside and opened his laptop.

He emailed Sibling Swap, explaining the situation. He liked Hari, he said, but wasn't sure how they could really be brothers who rode their bikes around and scoffed dough-nuts together. Hari seemed to prefer bugs. A Swap operative emailed back.

'Greetings, Swapper! We're sorry your latest brother was not massively suitable. We will hop on to arranging a new Swap! A replacement will be with you in the morning.'

Oh well, Jonny thought. He felt a weensy bit guilty about swapping Hari so quickly, but he was impatient to find his perfect brother match. He had to be out there, didn't he? Of course! Jonny knew it!

Hari didn't want to come in for dinner (he was snacking on a beetle instead), and Jonny couldn't persuade him to sleep indoors, so he took him a blanket then went upstairs to bed.

When Jonny woke the next morning, he looked out of his bedroom window. The blanket was lying on the grass. The sandpit was empty. Hari had gone.

CHAPTER THIRTEEN

THE PAST
PARTICIPATING

Jonny stared at the empty sandpit for a few moments, and then tiptoed out of his room. It was very early, his mum was in bed, but a sound made him pause on the stairs. It was a burp! A huge one!

He only knew one person who burped like that!

'Ted?' Jonny whispered.

Was he home?

Jonny peeped into the kitchen. There was no one there. He felt a tiny flash of disappointment, which was odd. It lasted just a second, though. He shrugged and poured himself some milk.

Back in his room, he was lying in bed with

his eyes closed when suddenly goosebumps prickled on his neck. He had the very strong and extremely unpleasant sense that he was being watched.

He told himself that was silly. Hari had left, Ted wasn't here and his mum was fast asleep. But the unnerving feeling carried on and …

Breathing! Jonny could definitely hear breathing.

Now the goosebumps spread down his arms like a pimply Mexican wave. Slowly, slowly, he opened his eyes and …

'MEUURRGGHH . . .!' Jonny said, in a half-screaming, half-choking sort of way.

A huge man was standing next to his bed with hands on hips and legs apart. He had a greyish look about him, but maybe that was just the weak early morning light.

The man leaned towards Jonny, his jewelled cape falling about his broad shoulders. A finger adorned with a giant ruby ring was pointing straight at him. He leaned so close that Jonny could make out a few grey hairs in his gingery beard and see his small eyes glinting angrily. Then Jonny noticed that he wasn't so much standing as floating, just a few centimetres off the floor.

'**BOO!**' said the man, before laughing so much the feather in his cap joggled. Then he looked around the room as if he had friends with him. There was no one there. Perhaps he was used to an audience?

'Did you see that?' he asked. 'Nearly peed his breeches! Look at him gawking! Come along, young squire! Be a man!'

'I'm only nine,' Jonny spluttered.

'Expect you've never seen a ghost before?'

Jonny shook his head.

'Never seen a king before, either,' said the man.

Jonny shook his head again.

'Queen?'

'No,' squeaked Jonny.

'Duke? Bishop?'

'Sorry, no,' said Jonny.

'Well, it's your lucky day! Henry the Eighth, Tudor king, English legend, at your service.'

Henry held out his hand for Jonny to shake, but when Jonny took it the hand melted into air.

'I'm Jonny,' said Jonny in a tiny, breathless voice. 'And you're Henry the Eighth's *ghost*?'

'The very same,' said Henry. 'Wondering how I got here?'

Jonny nodded rapidly. Henry sat down on the bed – well, hover-sat – and made himself comfy.

'I've got a man,' said Henry.

'A man?' whispered Jonny.

'Yes, he's a secretary.'

'A secretary man?'

'Yes, he's on the Other Side now, but I employed him when he was alive too. Thomas Cromwell. He was my master secretary. Very good at getting things done. You want a new wife but you're still married ... that kind of thing. He just –' Henry did an impatient little sweeping motion with his hand – 'sorts it out!'

'Oh,' was all Jonny could manage.

'Now, I had been in a bad temper about being dead for, ooh, a few hundred years at least. Not much fun, you see? I had tried to return to dear old England before, but it always ended pretty poorly. Everyone was terrified. So I says to Crommers, "I want to try the living world again – can you get me in?" And Crommers says, "There's a lad looking for a new brother. Open-minded little fellow. Not a bit bothered by ghosts, it says here on the application. Could Your Majesty do that?" "Of course," says I. I used to have a brother, although he died years ago. They all die, you know. Tragic really …'

Henry stroked his red beard thoughtfully for a moment. 'Anyway, that is how I come to be here before you. I am to be a brother. *Your* brother!'

Jonny was dumbstruck. He couldn't believe Henry was there, and he certainly didn't remember saying he was happy to have a ghost when he sent his form to Sibling Swap. What was going on?

'Do they have the internet in the afterlife?' he whispered, but Henry didn't seem to hear him.

'Methinks I shall make an excellent brother for you, young Nonny,' he said. 'I remember being a boy. Well, sort of. It was over five hundred years ago, after all! But I definitely have the impression that it was all jolly japes and wrestling and pie eating and the like. So huzzah for that! We shall have such sport.'

'Great!' said Jonny weakly.

'You don't sound very pleased,' said Henry, narrowing his eyes to menacing slits. 'Are you complaining? I hate complainers!'

'No! No! Sorry, Mr Sir Majesty Sir,' said Jonny.

'Good,' said Henry, cheerful again. 'You have nothing to fear. You're probably thinking Henry the Eighth, he's a king and immensely powerful and terrifying, et cetera. It's true, I used to be quite a tough customer, always chopping off people's heads and fighting the pope.'

He chuckled to himself. 'But, actually, I've

mellowed quite a bit in my old age. I'm more concerned with having fun than warring with the French or finding a new wife. That all rather took it out of me. I used to comfort eat, you know. Terrible really. Not good for one's waistline! Those wives would have me reaching for the mutton, I can tell you. I had six wives. *Six!* Not a lot of people know that.'

Jonny stared up at him, speechless, as Henry rambled on. He couldn't believe the ghost of Henry VIII was in his room. Or that this deceased king was supposed to fill the brother gap that Hari had created. What was Sibling Swap playing at? Jonny wasn't sure he wanted Henry VIII's ghost for a new brother, but what could he say? The guy was royalty!

'Now then!' said Henry. 'Stop looking so lily-livered and show me your manor house.

Come along now. Chop-chop! That's just my little jest! Geddit? Chop-chop! Chopping off heads? Oh, never mind.'

Jonny paused on the landing. 'My mum will be up soon,' he said, 'and ...'

'Never fear!' said Henry. 'Only you can see me. She won't be able to. I'll make sure of it. I can control who sees me and who doesn't. Just a little ghostly talent of mine. Told you I was a legend! Now, lead me to the cook's quarters. I'm famished.'

CHAPTER FOURTEEN

THE PHANTOM MENACE

Henry VIII yanked open the fridge door.

'Ah, yes, the victuals store!'

He rummaged inside.

'I'll just help myself to a morsel,' he said. 'Just something small. I can't manage to hold heavy things now I'm all ghostly. But a little something … Ah! What do we have here? Some form of posset?'

Henry grabbed a yoghurt and tipped it into his ghost mouth, gulped it down his ghost throat and **SLAP!** It fell straight through his ghost body and on to the floor.

'I've always enjoyed feasting,' he said. 'Appetite of a bear! But these days I can't seem to get enough sustenance!'

I can see why, thought Jonny, staring at the yoghurt splat on the floor. Widget spied it too, and began licking it up.

'Be gone, cur,' said Henry, kicking out at him.

'That's my dog!' shouted Jonny.

'Call that a hound?' snorted Henry.

'He's a Cockapoo.'

'Language!' said Henry. 'I won't tolerate a potty-mouthed child.'

'Sorry, it's the type of dog, Your Royal Mightiness,' said Jonny.

'Hmm,' said Henry, his top lip still curling with disdain. 'What does he do? Is he a good ratter? Is he fast? Can he take a deer?'

'He's good at catching a tennis ball,' offered Jonny.

'Tennis!' said Henry. 'I used to enjoy a game of that. Loved all sports, in fact. Marvellous for showing your true worth and valour. Actions speak louder than words, young Jimmy.'

'Jonny,' said Jonny.

'Now, show me to the great hall,' said Henry.

In the living room Henry stood and stared. His huge bulk almost filled the space.

'Not very grand,' he sniffed. 'You need some tapestries on the wall. Brighten the place up a bit.'

'Mum decorated in here last year,' said Jonny. 'The colour is a sort of white with a hint of –'

'And it's so *small*!' boomed Henry, striding around the room. 'How do you receive the court, foreign ambassadors, ladies-in-waiting?'

'We sometimes bring in a chair from the kitchen,' said Jonny, 'if we have family over …'

'What's this?' asked Henry, indicating the TV.

Jonny switched it on. There was a cartoon on. Henry's eyes grew wide. He looked behind the TV and even passed his hand through it

(Jonny still couldn't get over how totally mad this was).

'Why, this is pure alchemy,' Henry muttered. 'Spirits conjured from thin air ...'

He hover-sat on the floor, transfixed.

Jonny nipped back to the kitchen and quickly wiped the rest of the yoghurt up. His mum appeared silently.

'What are you doing?' she asked.

'Er, cleaning?' said Jonny.

'Ooh, lovely,' said his mum. 'Bless you! Such a good boy.'

Then she froze.

'What was that?' she asked.

She looked towards the living room. She'd heard a noise. Henry! He was guffawing as he watched the cartoon.

'I think the TV is on, that's all,' said Jonny, racing to the living room, where he frantic-ally waved at Henry to be quiet.

'What is it, lad?' asked Henry.

'My mum is in the kitchen ...' Jonny did the finger-across-the-throat gesture to urge Henry to shut up.

Henry's eyes squeezed into tiny dashes.

'Listen, my young sire,' he growled. 'If anyone is ordering any head chopping-off around here, it is me! Understand?'

'Of course, Your Utter Splendidness, I totally understand, but if you could just be a tiny weensy bit more quiet ...'

Unfortunately, Henry didn't keep quiet. Even with the noisy kettle boiling, Jonny could still hear him in the living room. Every time he hooted with laughter, Jonny had to laugh too, to cover it.

'What's so funny?' asked Jonny's mum.

'Just something I thought of,' said Jonny. 'To do with polar bears and scones and, er, you know? Hah, imagine that!'

Henry yelled again. 'God's bodkins! I've never seen the like of it!'

'Atishooo!' went Jonny, just a fraction too late.

'There! Again! I can hear something,' said his mum.

'I sneezed,' said Jonny.

'No, that shout,' she said.

'Next door?' suggested Jonny.

'Wait, what's that sound?' she said, staring at the kitchen door.

There was sort of whooshing noise. Coming up the hall. From the living room. They could both hear it.

Jonny gulped hard as Henry appeared in the kitchen. He winked at Jonny, then pointed with his ringed finger at the fridge before hovering towards it.

'Er, let's go and check in the living room,' said Jonny, grabbing his mum's hand

and dragging her up the corridor. 'Oh look, the TV *is* still on. That must be what we heard.'

Jonny snapped the TV off. His mum looked confused and slightly suspicious. Then Henry reappeared with another yoghurt. Jonny wasn't sure how this 'only you can see me' thing worked with Henry. What if Henry was invisible to his mum but the yoghurt wasn't? His mum was definitely not going to miss a mysterious floating yoghurt, and might have something to say about it too ... Uh oh ...

'I must go and get dressed,' said Jonny, racing past his mum and through Henry, who sort of ghosted around him like mist and then re-formed. Jonny grabbed the yoghurt as he went and held it up.

'Mmm, yoghurt!' he said. 'I'll eat it in my room!'

Then he jerked his head in a 'let's go' gesture to Henry and the regal phantom followed, drifting out through the living room wall and up through the ceiling. By the time Jonny made it to his bedroom, Henry was already there.

CHAPTER FIFTEEN

A DAY OF FUN – TUDOR-STYLE

Henry hover-sat on the swivel chair by Jonny's desk and spun round and round. He ate the yoghurt, which splatted through him and out on to the seat. Then he burped loudly and lobbed the pot over his shoulder. It hit the window and clattered to the floor.

'So we're going to be brothers,' said Jonny, sounding decidedly unsure. It had been a nutty few days, and now brother swapping seemed to have got even weirder.

'Why not?' said Henry, smiling. 'Are you ready for some brotherly fun? Two chaps up for a lark! What say you? The weather is fair. Shall we ride out?'

'On our bikes?' asked Jonny.

'Bikes? What? On our horses!' said Henry. 'Where are the stables?'

'We don't have stables or horses, sorry, Your Amazingness,' said Jonny. Henry glowered. Jonny shrunk back a little.

'No matter,' said Henry. 'We shall devise some other sport. How about archery?'

Henry disappeared through the bedroom wall and ghosted off towards the park. Jonny skipped downstairs, pulled on his shoes and quickly ran after him. Henry was the king, after all. You just kind of had to.

Using branches from a tree, the two fashioned a bow and then Henry whittled an arrow with a small knife he kept tucked inside his robes.

After seeing the king turn from jolly to angry and back again faster than Widget could eat ham, Jonny was surprised at how calm and patient Henry was. Jonny began to relax and enjoy himself. Soon he was shooting cans off a bench.

'Egad!' Henry roared as Jonny struck another one. 'That's the spirit.'

Jonny felt proud of Henry's praise – Ted always said he was rubbish at everything – and he felt cared for too. It had proved hard work being the older brother, looking out for Mervyn and trying to guess what Hari needed. But Henry was large and in charge, as only the ghost of a dead king from the sixteenth century can be.

In the afternoon Jonny took Henry to the Common, his favourite place. Henry knew lots about nature and hunting. He showed Jonny how to creep up on a duck, and explained how Widget might be trained to flush out deer. Ted just liked building dens here, which was good too, but an afternoon with Henry was much more adventurous. Before they left for home,

Jonny showed the dead king the dreaded Hanging Pants of Doom.

'There is nought to fear in those breeches,' snorted Henry when he saw them. 'Shoot them down with an arrow. Go on, lad!'

At first Jonny felt uneasy even looking at the pants, but soon he was pinging arrows at them. He didn't manage to shoot them out of the tree but it felt good to be facing up to them for once.

'Thanks for a lovely time, Your Spectacularness,' said Jonny as they sat in the kitchen in the late afternoon.

'It was enjoyable, wasn't it?' said Henry, his ghostly hand flying through Jonny's shoulder as he attempted to slap him heartily. 'Perhaps tomorrow we could joust, eh, Jeffrey?'

Jonny heard a key in the front door.

'That's my mum,' he said. 'Please, Your Royal Epicness, if you could just stay quietly upstairs for a while, I would be humbly grateful and everything, thank you so much, Your Lordship Sir.'

'Yes, yes,' said Henry. 'You know me ... quiet as a mouse!'

He roared with laughter then clapped his hand over his mouth.

'Sorry!' he whispered and winked at Jonny.

CHAPTER SIXTEEN

KING OF CHAOS

Jonny's mum appeared in the kitchen carrying some shopping bags.

'Did I hear a laugh again, or am I going mad?' she said, glancing around the room.

'Mad, I expect,' said Jonny.

Then Widget trotted into the room. He had an apple strapped to his head. Jonny's eyes grew wide at the sight. Henry hadn't stayed upstairs at all! In fact, there he was, ghosting along behind the dog, taking aim with the bow and arrow they'd made. Jonny shook his head, grimacing, trying to make Henry stop.

WHHEEEE!

The arrow flew across the room and straight out through an open window.

'Gah!' roared Henry.

'Who said that?' shrieked Jonny's mum. She grabbed a baguette from a shopping bag and brandished it like a sword.

'What's going on? Where are you?' she gasped, swinging the baguette. 'Get the phone, Jonny. I'm calling the police!'

'The police!' shrieked Jonny. 'I don't think we need to bother them, do we? They're probably busy.'

'There is somebody or something in here!' hissed Jonny's mum. 'Forget it! I'll use my mobile. You keep watch!'

She handed the baguette to Jonny while she rummaged in her bag for her phone. She had gripped the bread so hard there were nail marks in the crust.

While she spoke to the police, Jonny looked for Henry. Where had he gone?

'Hey nonny, nonny!' came a cry.

Jonny's mum dropped the phone and stared wildly around the room. Jonny could see Henry, of course. He was sitting on the kitchen table. And then Henry began to speak.

'Good day to you, madam,' he said. 'I can see you're rather alarmed, but no need to be upset. Awestruck, maybe, but not upset. Allow me to introduce myself.'

Then Jonny watched, horrified, as Henry did a sort of shiver, like a wet pigeon shaking off the rain, and turned from a faded ghost to a glowing, lifelike and extremely splendid figure – one that Jonny's mum was now staring at. His rich velvet robes glimmered, his jewels sparkled, his red hair gleamed. He was grinning too, and his teeth, Jonny noticed, were surprisingly white for someone over five hundred years old.

Jonny's mum gawped like she'd seen a ghost – which, to be fair, she had. Then she spluttered

something that sounded like 'Agaaaarrgg' and fainted.

'See? What did I tell you!' said Henry, looking disappointed. 'People tumble like plague victims at the sight of me.'

'Why did you have to do that?' Jonny screeched. 'Why did you have to make yourself visible to Mum?'

Henry had no time to answer. There was a hammering at the door.

'OPEN UP, IT'S THE POLICE!'

'The pope's niece?' said Henry.

BANG, BANG, BANG!

Jonny froze.

'We have received a 999 call from this address. Open up,' a policeman yelled through the letterbox.

Jonny tried to push Henry towards the back door, but his hands simply drifted through the king's ghostly form.

'Please leave!' said Jonny. 'You're amazing and it's been so cool meeting you and I'll really miss you, but you just made my mum faint and ...'

BANG, BANG, BANG!

'Now the police are here – the law! They're in charge, kind of. They sort out crime and bad stuff and take you away in handcuffs if you're naughty. If they see you, which they could now that you're all glowing and shiny,

I'll be in all kinds of trouble,' said Jonny, very fast and very urgently. 'They'll be shocked and scared and then it will be in the news and my mum will probably go mad at me and I'll get told off by the head teacher and we'll have TV crews and photographers and all sorts of people here and –'

'Peace, boy, I see your difficulties,' said Henry, smiling. 'I'll disappear again. You can trust me. Silent and invisible from three, two, one … Now!'

CHAPTER SEVENTEEN

AN INSPECTOR CALLS

Henry faded back to grey and ghosted off through the wall. Jonny took a deep breath, smoothed his hair and opened the door.

'We received a distress call from a woman at this property,' said the policeman.

'My mum fainted,' said Jonny.

'Dear, dear,' said the policeman. 'Not really my specialism, fainting.'

'She's OK now,' said Jonny. 'Thanks for coming. Sorry to have bothered you. Bye.'

But the policeman wouldn't go away. He wanted to come in and check on Jonny's mum. She had come to and was gasping about someone breaking in. The policeman took a few notes and looked all over the house, then he asked to check outside.

Jonny opened the back door for him. The policeman marched around the small garden, checking the fences and the shed.

'Nothing,' he said, 'but you ought to fix a lock on that shed. Anyone could get in!'

Finally, he left. Jonny sagged with relief. He'd felt sure Henry would fling a yoghurt at the policeman or fire an arrow at his hat, but true to his word, the royal guest had been silent and invisible. Jonny checked that his mum was resting quietly on the sofa, then went to find Henry. He was lying on Jonny's bed.

'I think, Your Wonderfulness, that it might be best if you return to the Other Side,' said Jonny nervously.

'But we were going to be brothers!' said Henry, sitting up and pouting.

'I know,' said Jonny. 'I just don't think it's going to work.'

'Am I too Tudor?' asked Henry. 'Too regal? Too old-fashioned? Too fabulous?'

'Too *dead*!' blurted Jonny. 'You're a ghost! You died, like, ages ago! Sorry. You're also really great and fun, but I just want a normal brother who is alive and roughly my age and doesn't make people faint or call the police.'

Jonny half expected the dead king to roar angrily at him, but instead Henry reached his ghostly hand out and laid it on Jonny's shoulder. It floated straight through it.

'We had some larks, though, eh, Jonty?'

'Jonny,' muttered Jonny.

'Indeed,' said Henry. 'Perhaps we'll meet again some day. I hope you find the brother you want. Better luck next time, eh? That's what they used to say to me about wives. I had six you know. *Six!*'

With that, Henry faded to grey and disappeared.

Jonny sat at his desk and emailed the Sibling Swap operatives again. He explained that all the swaps so far had been a bit peculiar, from ghosts to mythical creatures to a boy raised by meerkats, and asked if this was just how the website worked.

A Swap operative emailed back.

'Apologies, Swapper, for the unsatisfactory new brother. We have checked your original application form and you had not ticked the box requesting only HUMAN brothers. We keep a small number of non-human swaps on our books to offer the greatest variety to our Swappers.'

So that's why the brother swaps have been weird, Jonny thought. *That explains everything!* It was just a simple error he'd made on the form ... *Oh, relief times five trillion!*

'Can I tick that human box now, please?' Jonny typed.

'Sure!' the Swap op replied. 'We have a massive choice of *human* brothers and will have a replacement with you tomorrow morning. There's no stopping the swapping until we get it right!'

Jonny closed the laptop. What a day! His faith in Sibling Swap had been wobbling there for a bit. Then he remembered tomorrow was bank holiday Monday. Bonus brother-bonding time! He sighed deeply and smiled. It was all going to be just fine!

Before bed, Jonny finished work on an enormous brick castle that he and Ted had begun together in a rare afternoon of brotherly harmony. It had sat on his bedroom floor ever since, like a shrine to good brother times. Sometimes, Jonny remembered, he and Ted did have fun together. Not very often, it's true, but sometimes.

Next morning Jonny was woken by the doorbell. It was brother number four.

CHAPTER EIGHTEEN

ALFIE ARRIVES

Jonny pulled the door open. A boy stood on the front step. He beamed at Jonny, blue eyes twinkling, golden hair gleaming, cuteness radiating from him like water off a shaking dog.

'I'm Alfie!' said the little chap. He only came up to Jonny's shoulder. 'Come from the Sibling Swap!'

'Hello! How old are you?' Jonny asked.

'Eight,' said Alfie. 'But I'm nearly nine.'

'Perfect! I'm nearly ten,' said Jonny. 'Now, before you come in, can I just check: you look human. Are you?'

Alfie looked confused.

'Are you a regular boy?' Jonny continued. 'Not one raised by porcupines? You're not some sort of weird fairytale creature that was brought up on a glacier by griffins?'

'What are you on about?' Alfie asked.

'You're not a pixie, are you? Or a werewolf? Or allergic to air or happiest living in a bog or ...'

Alfie shook his head.

'Excellent!' said Jonny. 'Come on in! Be my guest!'

'I'm not your guest, though, am I!' laughed Alfie, stepping inside. 'I'm your new brother! You asked for me and here I am! Race you to the top of the stairs!'

Alfie shot upstairs like he'd been fired out of a cannon, with Jonny behind him. Once inside Jonny's room, Alfie climbed on to the bed.

'Let's see who can bounce on the bed the best!' he said.

'You're on!' said Jonny, and immediately

the two boys got stuck into some rip-roaring bouncing. What a great way to break the ice with your new brother! Eventually, panting and giggling, they flopped down on the duvet.

'Phew, that was fun,' Jonny puffed. 'You're a good bouncer. Have you bounced before?'

'Of course!' said Alfie. 'I love bouncing. And running around. And climbing trees and doing ninja rolls off swings and –'

'I get it,' said Jonny. 'Me too. Except for the climbing bit. I just like, you know, messing about. My older brother, Ted, says that's stupid. He wouldn't even play cards with me. He says, "You know I'll win, so what's the point? I'm better at everything."'

'He sounds annoying,' said Alfie.

Yeah, he was pretty annoying, thought Jonny, *the way he always went on about how hard it was being the oldest because he had to get up early for school and walk the dog sometimes ...* 'Hey, where are you going?'

Alfie had shot out the door. As he ran, one foot clipped the brick castle on the floor, knocking off a turret. Jonny found him in Ted's bedroom, looking through the wardrobe. Jonny noticed with a gulp that it was still full of Ted's clothes. Had Ted not packed before he left? Perhaps there hadn't been time ... Then he saw that Alfie had put on Ted's favourite hoodie. It was gigantic on him. With the hood up he could hardly see out. He stumbled about the room, tripping on the bed and bouncing off the walls.

Jonny laughed. Then he grabbed Ted's school tie and put it on.

'Ooh, look, my name's Ted and I'm really cool because I go to secondary school. We have design lessons and do trampolining! Did I mention I'm nearly thirteen years old?

Hey, check out my mobile phone. It's so smart! It's a smartphone! You've only got a rubbish brick thing, Jonny. Durr, what a loser!'

Alfie was squealing with laughter.

'I'm glad I make you laugh,' said Jonny. 'It was tricky to make Ted laugh. He said I wasn't funny!'

'You are quite funny,' said Alfie.

'Yeah? Well, if you think that's only *quite* funny, wait until you see this!'

He ran back to his room, pulled on his panda onesie and stuffed it with all his teddies (despite being almost ten, Jonny still liked his soft toys, which was yet another thing Ted teased him about). Then he lumbered towards Alfie, looking like a sumo wrestler who had eaten all his friends' pies.

Alfie laughed and laughed at this, then ran at Jonny, power-jumping head first into his massive stuffed belly until they both collapsed on the floor.

'That was good,' Alfie said. 'I'm probably funnier, though.'

Jonny didn't say anything. He had unzipped his onesie and was busy pulling teddies from deep inside it.

'Was Ted really like that?' Alfie asked. 'Like your impression of him? He was next door to me at Sibling Swap, but I didn't get to know him.'

'Next door?' asked Jonny.

'Yes, in the place the siblings wait,' said Alfie. 'The fishy-smelling place.'

Jonny paused. It felt weird to know Alfie had been near Ted recently, that Ted was being held somewhere, waiting for a new brother or sister to snap him up. Jonny's tummy did an uneasy little flutter.

'Well?' said Alfie. 'Was Ted like you said?'

'Oh yes,' said Jonny. 'He always said I was slow at everything and called me a human sloth. And he liked to sit in here all the time messing about on his phone, which was so boring. He also changed his name in the contacts on my phone from Ted to GOD! Really annoying. Sometimes we had a nice time, I suppose. We made that castle together, the one in my room ...'

'Are you coming down for breakfast?' Jonny's mum called from downstairs.

'Come and meet my mum!' said Jonny.

'She's my mum now, as well,' said Alfie.

Jonny blinked, processing this for a second. It felt a bit weird. He'd forgotten the whole mother–son side of this brother swapping. He would have to share his mum with a new brother.

'Bet she thinks I'm cute,' said Alfie. 'All grown-ups do! Just watch.'

CHAPTER NINETEEN

ADVENTURES WITH A LOVELY LITTLE CHAP

Alfie was right.

'And who's this?' Jonny's mum asked when she saw Alfie. He had tucked in behind Jonny, like he was terribly shy, and was now peeping round at Jonny's mum, smiling cutely, his blond hair shimmering like a Saharan sunset.

'This is Alfie,' said Jonny. 'My ... er ...'

'Hello!' said Alfie, his huge manga eyes pulling her in like impossible-to-resist tractor beams.

'Is Alfie playing here today?' Jonny's mum asked. 'I hope so. Will you stay, Alfie?'

'I'd really love to, yes, please, if that's OK, thanks,' said Alfie, beaming again.

'Maybe he could sleep over as well?' Jonny suggested. 'Ted texted to say he'll be at Jim's again tonight, as it's a bank holiday and all that …'

'Great!' said Jonny's mum. 'How about you two go to the park after breakfast?'

The boys nodded.

'I think this calls for a special treat, don't you?' Jonny's mum added, looking at Alfie like he was a basket of kittens. 'It's nice to have a new friend here, isn't it, Jonny? What's your favourite thing to eat, Alfie?'

Jonny whispered 'doughnuts' into Alfie's ear and gave him a nudge with his elbow.

'Go nuts!' shouted Alfie.

'He means doughnuts!' blurted Jonny. 'It's his funny word for them.'

'Doughnuts? Jonny loves those too,' said his mum. 'Buy a big box, Jonny. After all, it's not often we have such a lovely little chap to visit.'

After cornflakes, Jonny went outside with the lovely little chap, and the lovely little chap proceeded to run up and down the pavement at top speed, whooping and whacking trees with a stick in a manner quite opposite to the way a *real* lovely little chap might behave.

'I betted that she would love me,' said Alfie. 'And I betted right. Your mum totally thinks I'm amazing. I bet she loves me more than you!'

'Of course she doesn't,' said Jonny, trying to sound confident. 'Don't be daft. I'm her real son, anyway.'

'Yeah, but I'm really cute,' said Alfie, stamping on a snail.

'Hyper, more like,' Jonny muttered under his breath. He was having fun with Alfie, for sure, but the pace was a little hectic. Then Jonny's fingers felt the coins in his pocket and he remembered the doughnuts that

Alfie's charm had helped secure. Suddenly, he felt better.

Jonny marched off towards the shop with Alfie racing around him, now beating bins and lamp posts with his stick like a demented gibbon.

'Hello, Mrs Algernon,' said Jonny politely, when he saw his neighbour pruning her privet hedge. Mrs Algernon just nodded at him. Yup, still grumpy. Probably hadn't forgiven him for falling into it the other day. Probably never would.

Jonny hadn't seen Mrs Algernon smile in the five years they had lived near each other. Ted said she didn't know how to smile. 'Her face has all the muscle tone of porridge,' Ted would say. That always made Jonny laugh.

Mrs Algernon squinted at him and gruffly nodded again, then she spotted Alfie and her face seemed to melt, like cheese on a radiator.

'New friend?' she asked Jonny.

'This is Alfie,' he said.

By now Alfie was standing next to Jonny, in full shy, adorable mode. *Wow*, thought Jonny, *this kid really knows how to turn on the charm. Look at him go! He could get an award for that performance! He just totally knows how to win over grown-ups!*

'Very nice to meet you,' said Alfie, doing a little bow crossed with a curtsey. It would have looked ridiculous had Jonny done it, but, of course, when Alfie did it, it was pure, solid gold, one hundred per cent charm. With a cherry on top. No, two cherries, actually. And a tiny umbrella.

That was game over for Mrs Algernon. She was smitten. Alfie's full-on cute offensive had claimed another victim. Jonny was impressed.

'How delightful,' she said. And then she smiled. She *actually* smiled!

Jonny thought he might faint or pee his pants or spontaneously combust. *Unreal!* he thought, *I have to tell Ted about this!* And then, *Oh, yeah, he's not here ...*

'We have to go,' said Jonny, giving Alfie a little shove. 'Off to buy doughnuts.'

Mrs Algernon turned back to Jonny.

Instantly, her smile slipped away, her eyes darkened and her face seemed to close, like someone slamming down the shutters on a shop full of rainbows.

'She really liked you!' said Jonny as the two boys walked along. 'How do you do that?'

Alfie shrugged. 'Old ladies in particular think I'm lovely. Bet I've made her day. Probably even her whole entire month! She totally prefers me to you now!'

'Yeah, yeah,' said Jonny, feeling just a teensy bit annoyed at how competitive and confident Alfie was. It was all a bit exhausting. The boy had so much energy too. He could barely stand still or shut up. Or could he? Jonny tried a little experiment.

'Can you be quiet?' he asked Alfie. 'Just until we walk to the shop.'

'Being quiet is boring, though,' said Alfie, poking his stick into a drain.

'OK, how about this,' said Jonny. 'A challenge! I bet you can't shut up for two minutes!'

That was more like it. At the suggestion of a bet, Alfie perked up.

'Eeeeeaasy!' he roared. 'Two minutes? Bet I can. I totally can.'

'OK, I'll time you,' said Jonny.

And he did. And Alfie shut his mouth and concentrated on not making a peep. It was a lovely, quiet two minutes in which Jonny watched tiny Alfie, his cheeks going red with the effort of not speaking, and thought, *Ahh, you're kind of fun and cute, aren't you, especially when you're not yelling* ... But all too soon the time was up and the yelling was on again.

'I win!' Alfie roared, and began running around whacking more things with his stick. 'Win! Win! Win the thing! *Winner!*'

CHAPTER TWENTY

A LARK IN THE PARK

The boys bought the doughnuts from Charlie in the corner shop. Charlie was very impressed by Alfie too, and ruffled his hair affectionately. Mind you, Charlie did that with everyone, even grown-ups sometimes. He was just a nice, friendly guy.

Jonny got twelve doughnuts, iced in a rainbow of tempting colours and lined up neatly in a box with a see-through lid.

'I really love doughnuts,' said Jonny, admiring them.

'Me too,' said Alfie.

The two were quiet for a moment, happily gazing at the sugary, greasy treats. Then ...

'Bet I can eat more doughnuts in one go than you!' said Alfie.

'That's a risky bet,' said Jonny. 'You risk being sick. I hate being sick. It's one of my least favourite things. Here's a better bet for you. Bet I can beat you to the park gate. Go!'

The boys bombed towards the gate, Jonny just making it before Alfie.

'I win!' said Jonny. 'Whoop!'

Alfie glared at him and then ran into the park.

'Bad loser!' Jonny muttered. Then he remembered Ted calling him that. They'd been playing a game of cards and Ted was thrashing him, and eventually Jonny got so frustrated he threw the cards. They sprayed across the kitchen like autumn leaves in a wind tunnel, mostly landing in Widget's water bowl.

A shout from Alfie on the swings grabbed Jonny's attention.

'Look at me!' he called. 'Bet you can't go this high!'

Alfie was standing up, swinging in insanely huge and dangerous arcs.

Jonny began swinging alongside him. The two went higher and higher, whooping for joy.

'Bet you can't jump off!' shouted Alfie, and before Jonny could answer, Alfie flung himself from the sweeping swing and rolled across the grass.

'I'm fine!' he said, hopping up. 'I did a ninja roll! Try it!'

So Jonny tried a ninja roll off the swing too, and nearly rolled straight through a family's picnic.

Next, the two boys tackled the roundabout. By now Alfie was fizzing like a vitamin tablet in a glass of Pixie Fizz. He began spinning it madly, while Jonny lay on it, staring at the sky, screaming with laughter. This was more like it! Fun. Proper, nice, fun-packed fun. Two brothers, mucking about in the park. Perfect!

After ten minutes of high-speed spinning, the two boys sat dizzily on the grass, catching their breath. Jonny was tired, but Alfie wasn't done yet. Like an extreme-sports nut planning his next daredevil parachute dive off a skyscraper while still in the middle of his current daredevil parachute dive off a skyscraper, Alfie had other challenges in his sights. He was staring at a tall tree.

'Bet I can climb to the top of that tree!' he said, his blue eyes lighting up like gas flames.

'Forget it!' said Jonny, looking over. 'It's way too high.'

'Bet I can!' said Alfie.

'Well, I don't want to have to rescue you if you get stuck. I don't really like climbing,' said Jonny. He stared up at the tree. 'Besides, it's really massive. Don't try to climb it. Not a good idea.'

'No, you're right, it's not a good idea,' said Alfie. Jonny felt pleased for a second. Alfie had listened to him.

'Climbing that tree is not a good idea,' Alfie continued. 'It is an *awesome* idea!'

CHAPTER TWENTY-ONE

BETTING COMES BEFORE A FALL

Before Jonny could say 'Wait!' or 'No' or 'Ummm …' Alfie was off. He clambered up the tree at top speed, like a squirrel late for his dentist appointment. Jonny jogged over with the box of doughnuts and gazed up. It really was a very big tree indeed.

Seconds later, Alfie was near the top, clinging to the branches, which were swaying in the wind.

'Woo-hoo!' Alfie yelled. 'I knew I could do it. Nearly at the top! I'm going to win the bet! Are you coming up too?'

I didn't actually bet you, Jonny thought, feeling exasperated by Alfie's endless bets and challenges. *And no, I don't want to climb up too, thanks. I already told you I don't like climbing.*

Jonny stayed where he was, feet firmly on the ground, but Alfie kept taunting him from above.

'Come on, Jonny, climb up,' he yelled. 'It's super fun!'

'Oh all right,' said Jonny eventually. Anything to shut Alfie up. Plus Alfie was younger than him. Older brothers had to be better at stuff than younger brothers, didn't they? That was the natural order of things. Jonny was the oldest now, so ...

He tried to swing his legs up over the lowest branch, and just managed to heave himself up. Then he glanced up at Alfie, who had now made it to the very top. He could barely see the little boy's face, but he suddenly sensed that something was wrong.

'Do you want to come down now?' Jonny asked. Perhaps Alfie would make another bet, about how fast he could descend, but instead, in a small voice, he just said, 'Can't.'

'What?' shouted Jonny.

'I can't get down,' Alfie said limply. He was clinging to the uppermost branch, which was now swaying in the wind even more.

'Oh massive swear word,' muttered Jonny.

What should he do? He had some experience of protecting his new brothers. He had made sure Henry wasn't seen by the police, and he'd tried to save Mervyn from the pond and the puddle (OK, without success, but it's the thought that counts). Jonny wasn't afraid of water, but climbing up there after Alfie? That was something else! He knew he wasn't a good enough climber. Ted would have been able to rescue him. Ted was amazing at climbing. If only Ted were …

CRACK!

The branch Alfie was standing on began to give way.

'You need to start climbing down, Alfie, NOW!' shouted Jonny.

'But …' spluttered Alfie. He was now wobbling on the unsteady branch.

Jonny dropped to the ground and ran to where he could see Alfie better. Peering up, he could tell that the slim branch Alfie was standing on would soon break.

'Climb down, Alfie!' he yelled.

Too late. With another loud **CRACK**, the branch snapped and Alfie fell.

It was like watching a tiny blond cherub plummeting from heaven. Jonny gasped but he didn't panic. He spotted the box of doughnuts and, with a firm kick, sent it skittering across the grass. Alfie fell, fell, fell. The doughnuts skidded and stopped

and almost immedi-
ately – **THUMP!**
Alfie landed squarely
on the box.

The fall winded
him, but the soft
cushiony doughnuts
saved him. He was
fine. Breathless and
bruised, but fine.
The doughnuts, on
the other hand, were
not. They looked
like doughnut road-
kill. And Jonny? He
was wide-eyed with
shock.

'Told you I could
climb to the top of
the tree,' said Alfie,

standing up and rubbing his back.

Jonny said nothing. He was shaking. It's not every day you see your brother fall out of a tree. A really big tree.

'Wow, you could have, like, hurt yourself,' Jonny stuttered. 'Are you OK? Thank goodness for the doughnuts.'

'I would have been fine, anyway,' said Alfie, shrugging. 'I would have done another cool ninja roll or something.'

Jonny pulled a 'really' face, and then, without asking, Alfie opened the box, peeled a flattened doughnut off the bottom of it and stuffed it into his mouth.

Jonny watched in silence as Alfie chomped. Despite loving doughnuts, he had lost his appetite.

CHAPTER TWENTY-TWO

THOUGHTS ON BROTHER SWAPPING

Jonny was glad to watch some TV after lunch. After all the excitement in the park he wanted to relax. Alfie, on the other hand, didn't seem to grasp the concept of relaxing. He flicked through the DVD collection, took the batteries out of the remote control, pulled feathers out of the cushions and tickled Widget's nose with them. He hardly seemed to notice the screen. Jonny sighed and turned it off.

'Bedtime,' he said.

'But it's only five o'clock, and I haven't had any dinner yet!' said Alfie.

'I'll ask Mum to bring you a sandwich,'

Jonny said. 'We often have an early night and a sandwich in bed in this house. Get used to it. Anyway, you must be tired. I bet you are!'

'Bet I'm not!' Alfie said, doing a couple of star jumps to prove it.

Alfie was wrong, though. He was one of those kids that runs around all day like an ant who's training for a triathlon, but when finally placed between a mattress and a duvet, falls asleep instantly. Just like that!

After seeing Alfie power down like a disconnected screen, Jonny sighed and went to bed too. He lay with his eyes shut and thought about Alfie. He told himself Alfie would work out as his brother. He was certain of it. Well, maybe certain was pushing it a bit. Sure. That was better. Jonny felt *sure* Alfie would work out. They'd had fun together in the park, after all. And at least Alfie wasn't like Ted, who almost never joined in with Jonny's games and preferred teasing him about touching the Hanging Pants of Doom. So, it had all been great, in fact. Apart from the bit when Alfie fell out of the tree. Apart from that. But, yes, Jonny was sure he could make it work. Well, confident. Confident-ish ... OK, he was *reasonably* confident that Alfie would make a good brother. Who never sat still to watch TV ... And who had no understanding of danger or risk or ...

Jonny's eyes pinged open. He stared at the ceiling. He remembered the moment Alfie fell out of the tree and he felt slightly sick. Would he always have to keep an eye on Alfie in future? Was that what being an older brother involved? Jonny didn't want that! He never had to look after Ted. Then Jonny thought about how energetic Alfie was, always bouncing about like an eager spaniel desperate to have his ball thrown. At least Ted gave Jonny some space. Ted spent time in his room, so Jonny could enjoy hanging out with his mum or drawing at the kitchen table. And at the end of the day, the three of them would sit and watch TV together, quietly ...

Jonny got out of bed and sat at his desk. He made a new sign for the door, to replace the one saying OLDER BROTHERS KEEP OUT. This one said ALL BROTHERS KEEP OUT. Then he began reconstructing the brick castle that Alfie had kicked, the one he and Ted had made all those months ago. It seemed like weeks since Jonny had last seen Ted. In fact, it had only been a few days.

CHAPTER TWENTY-THREE

COMPETITIVE CORNFLAKES

The next morning Jonny woke up with a weight on his chest and cheese in his ears.

'Would you like some cheese from me? Would you like some cheese from me? Because MY CHEESE is the best!'

Alfie was straddling Jonny, pinning him to the mattress as he sang a ridiculous song about cheese.

'Morning!' said Alfie. 'Bet you're awake!'

'I am now!' huffed Jonny. 'What *are* you thinking? It's six thirty! And there's a sign on the door. Can't you read?'

'I was bored,' said Alfie. 'Can we have

breakfast? Bet I can eat a bigger bowl of cereal than you!'

'Are you really making a bet with me, at half past six on a Tuesday morning, about who can eat more cereal?' groaned Jonny.

Alfie nodded fast.

'Seriously?' said Jonny.

He tried to roll over and go back to sleep, but Alfie kept poking him. Then he began prizing open Jonny's eyelids with his tiny fingers. This felt extremely unpleasant. It was the final straw.

'Get OFF!' shouted Jonny, shoving Alfie on to the floor. He got out of bed and stood there, panting a little. His fists were clenched. His eyes were shining. Something had flipped inside him.

'You want to bet me? About cereal? Right here, right now?' Jonny said.

Alfie nodded, half excited, half nervous.

'OK, fine. I'm in. Let's do this, brother. Bring. It. On. It's going to be fun, isn't it? And fun is good. Fun is the best! Fun is what you're supposed to have with your brother. So let's go. Absolutely. What are you waiting for?'

Alfie jumped up, looking slightly confused by Jonny's strange, wide-eyed eagerness.

'I bet I can eat more cereal than you. I'm nearly nine you know!' he said, following Jonny out of the room. But on the stairs Jonny stopped suddenly and turned to face his tiny competitive brother.

'Just one thing,' Jonny said. 'If I win, you never bet me again. Ever!'

'OK ...' said Alfie, sounding a bit uncertain, but only for a split second. 'But I *will* win!'

In the kitchen Jonny measured out corn-flakes into two bowls, pouring out equal amounts of milk and setting the kitchen timer.

'One minute to clear the bowl, starting ...'

Alfie grabbed his spoon, his baby-blue eyes looking suddenly steely.

'Now!'

Both boys attacked their cereal. Their spoons were a blur. Milk splattered their faces and their jaws jumped up and down as they demolished the cornflakes. Jonny was fast, but – giant, really colourful swear word!

– Alfie was quicker. His mouth looked like a hamster's, rapid-fire chewing the food, turning it into cornflake mush and swallowing it.

DING-A-LING-A-LING!

The boys threw down their spoons. Alfie had cleared his bowl. Jonny still had a few flakes floating at the bottom in a puddle of milk.

'Ooof!' said Alfie, doing some kind of victory gesture that looked faintly rude. 'Told you I could beat you! I win the bet!'

'Best of three!' said Jonny. He couldn't quite believe he was doing this. A cornflake-eating competition at 6.30 a.m.? Madness! But Alfie's restless energy and need to compete had pushed Jonny to the brink. If Alfie was to work out as his brother, Jonny had to show him who was boss, and prove he was the oldest and the best. He had to fight, conquer, WIN! And, hopefully, shut Alfie up once and for all.

Jonny refilled the bowls, poured the milk, reset the timer and they were off again.

This time Jonny shovelled as fast as he could, barely breathing between mouthfuls. When the timer went, he dropped his spoon and gasped for air. He had done it! His bowl was empty. He glanced at Alfie's. There were still some cornflakes left in it.

'Beat you!' shouted Jonny. 'Ha! I did it! You got owned! Beaten!'

'There's still one more round,' said Alfie.

Both boys now looked grimly determined. This was the decider. Jonny had never felt more competitive in his life. The fate of his whole existence, his home, the town he lived in, the very world seemed to be resting on this final bowl.

Jonny set the timer again, gripped his spoon and ...

'Go!' he shouted.

They plunged their spoons into their third bowl of cornflakes. Jonny's jaw ached but he was determined to win. He glanced at Alfie and was delighted to see him slowing down. Then Alfie clutched his stomach and dropped his spoon with a clatter on the floor. Jonny looked up, just in time to see Alfie open his mouth and let out an enormous ...

BUUURRRPPPP!

The blast hit Jonny in the face. It was so powerful it seemed to blow him backwards in his chair. Powerful, and also damp. It smelled of milk and mashed cornflakes. There was even a whiff of yesterday's doughnuts in there too. *Disgusting*, Jonny thought, and his body agreed. He raced upstairs to the bathroom and was sick. Outside the door he could hear Alfie laughing.

'Did you just throw up?' he said. 'Excellent! You know what that means? I win the bet.'

CHAPTER TWENTY-FOUR

OPERATION OUTSMART

Jonny sat miserably on the bathroom floor. Alfie had laughed when he'd been sick. That wasn't kind. Then he remembered, with a sigh, that Ted was often not particularly kind either. Maybe this was just how brothers were? What would Ted have done if Jonny had barfed up his cornflakes? Laughed too, perhaps, but after laughing Ted would have asked him how he was or helped him to bed, wouldn't he?

Jonny remembered the time he fell off his bike trying to ride through a stream. Ted had told him he could do it, even though he probably knew it was impossible. The stream was too deep. Jonny's bike was too small.

He cycled in about halfway and then fell sideways into the muddy water. But after nearly peeing his pants with laughter, Ted had lent Jonny his jumper and helped him pull his bike out of the mud. Because your brother, however mean, is still your brother, right?

Alfie, on the other hand, didn't seem to care about anything except making bets and winning and trying to prove that he was the best despite being only eight. Last night Jonny had gone from certain to sure to reasonably confident that he could make life with Alfie work. This morning, though, he was no longer certain, sure or reasonably confident about anything.

Then he heard his mum knock softly on the door.

'Jonny?' she asked. 'Let me in, darling, so I can help you.'

He opened the door and saw Alfie grinning up at her.

'I beat him in a cornflake-eating race!' said Alfie proudly, but Jonny's mum wasn't interested. She was hugging Jonny. He thought he might cry. He suddenly realised he had also been worrying that his mum might prefer Alfie, that Alfie's cutie-pieness might lure her away from her true son. Now, with a tidal wave of relief, he knew this wouldn't happen.

Jonny's mum suggested he go back to bed for a bit. But, shortly after snuggling down, Alfie burst in.

'You can't beat me at eating, at climbing trees, at jumping, at being annoying by singing the cheese song ...' said Alfie, counting his achievements off on his tiny fingers while Jonny gazed at him, realising, slowly but surely, that Alfie didn't really care about him or his feelings, or anything other than proving he was the best, and charming adults so he could get away with all sorts of nonsense.

'Why did you end up on Sibling Swap?' Jonny interrupted, but deep down he'd already guessed why. He could have put a bet on it, in fact. 'Did you annoy your brother so much he put you on the site?'

'Sister,' said Alfie, but he was hardly listening. 'Anyway, I can probably beat you at tons of other things too, like long jump or ...'

Yes, but I can beat you at thinking, Jonny decided, remembering how he had tricked Alfie into shutting up by making it a bet. *You may be able to charm Mrs Algernon, you may be agile, you may have nine lives, but I have something you don't. Brains! If I can't beat you, I can at least outsmart you, just like a proper older brother!*

With that, Jonny sat up.

'You're probably right,' he said. 'You probably can beat me at everything. Like jumping on the sofa. I mean, I can only jump up and down on it twenty times in a minute, but I bet you can do more.'

'I bet I can too!' shouted Alfie, rushing down to the living room and pinging about on the sofa in a frenzy. Jonny followed him and watched passively. He wasn't even counting.

'Nice! Amazing! You win. You're better at jumping than me,' said Jonny. 'Oh my goodness, I've just realised. I bet you're better at running up and down stairs than me.'

Before he'd even finished the sentence Alfie was hurling himself up and down the stairs, over and over again. Jonny congratulated him and issued another bet, and another and another, each one more tantalising than the last. Vaulting the garden wall. Leapfrogging the wheelie bin. Jumping, hopping, catching a ball. Whatever Jonny challenged Alfie to do, he did. He was so competitive that he even cleaned the toilet in under forty-five seconds, just because Jonny said it would take him fifty.

After half an hour of incessant betting, Alfie was growing tired, but Jonny wouldn't let up.

'This is so fun!' he lied. 'You really are good at everything. And you're only eight! I can't believe it.'

Alfie nodded and beamed and puffed a bit, his pretty cheeks flushed pink from the exertion.

'Oh no, hang on!' said Jonny. 'I've just realised something you can't do.'

'What?' said Alfie.

'I bet you can't run all the way back to Sibling Swap.'

'Easy!' roared Alfie. 'It's only a little way away. Super, mega, extra easy!'

'So you know where Sibling Swap is?'

'Yup, I can find it,' said Alfie. 'It's in a warehouse on the edge of town, over there.'

He pointed through the window and Jonny squinted in the same direction.

'Sorry, no, I've made a mistake,' said Jonny, shaking his head. 'You can't run all the way over there. I know you're really fast, but that's just too far.'

'I *can*,' said Alfie. 'In fact, I bet I could run there in ten minutes.'

'What?' said Jonny. 'Only ten minutes? No, sorry, it's impossible. I bet you can't.'

'Can! Can! Can!' Alfie said, pogoing from one foot to the other.

'No way,' said Jonny. 'It cannot be done.'

'It can! I can do it!' shrieked Alfie, looking like he might burst.

Jonny was silent for a moment, and then smiled calmly at him. 'Go on then,' he said.

That was it. Jonny didn't need to say it again. It was like he'd shot the starter pistol for the Olympic 100 metre race. Alfie was gone, speeding out of the front door and down the street as fast as his almost-nine-year-old legs would carry him.

Jonny watched the tiny figure disappear into the distance, and then he emailed the Sibling Swap office, telling them to expect Alfie on their doorstep very soon. He added that he didn't want another swap right away. He needed time to think about it all. Soon after, a Swap op emailed back to say he was entitled to a replacement anyway, and they had already sent one. Jonny sighed and then shrugged. *You know what they say?* he thought. *Fifth time lucky.* Then he realised that, actually, nobody ever said that. Oh well …

CHAPTER TWENTY-FIVE

BROTHER NUMBER FIVE

Jonny was glad to go to school. His mum suggested he take the day off, after being sick, but he felt relieved to have swapped Alfie and keen to get back to something close to normal life. After an eventful weekend of brother swapping, it was good to see his friends again.

'How is it going?' George asked when the two boys were alone. 'With your new brother?'

'Brothers, more like,' Jonny said. 'It's not gone quite to plan. I've had more than one.'

'What, like four or something?' said George.

Jonny paused, counted on his fingers and looked at George. 'How did you guess?' he said. 'Yes, I've had four and the fifth is coming later. I don't know, George, it feels quite tricky.

I've been sent a lot of funny matches and it's quite hard work. You're lucky not having any brothers or sisters. Much simpler!'

George looked a little worried and patted his friend's arm, then the two of them went into class.

School was a busy, happy distraction from brother-related problems, but as Jonny walked home later that day his thoughts turned to Sibling Swap again. Who would the Swap ops send him this time? He crossed his fingers and hoped hard that the next brother would also be the final one.

Jonny hadn't been home long when the doorbell rang. There was a new brother standing there, with a bag over his shoulder. He was taller than Jonny, with dark hair. He had big brown eyes, like a beautiful Jersey cow, but their expression was sulky, cross and a tiny bit scary.

'I'm Pete,' he said. 'From Sibling Swap.'

'Great!' said Jonny. 'Come in.' Then, just to be sure Pete wasn't Alfie mark II, he added, 'Bet you can't throw that bag all the way to the end of the hall.'

Pete frowned. 'It's OK,' he said. 'I'll carry it.'

Phew! thought Jonny, *Now time to check his age. He looks a bit older than me.*

'I'm nine,' said Pete.

'Me too!' said Jonny. 'But I'm nearly ten, in about four weeks.'

'My birthday is ages away,' said Pete.

Great! thought Jonny. *We're both nine and, even though Pete is much bigger than me, I am actually older than him. This is all working out well so far.*

'This is my mum,' said Jonny, introducing them as she came out of the kitchen. 'Is it OK if Pete stays the night? Maybe he could have Ted's room?'

'It's Tuesday. Isn't Ted back from school?' she asked.

'No,' said Jonny.

He was desperately trying to think of another reason for Ted being absent.

'No?' said his mum.

'Yes,' said Jonny.

'Yes or no?'

'Ted went on that trip thing, didn't he? It started today and runs all week. The school organised it.'

Jonny's mum looked blank.

'It's that adventure sports and pastry-making residential thing. They all go on it in year eight. Maybe Dad got the letter about it.'

Jonny's mum frowned.

'Really?' she sighed. 'I'll check the school website later. Wish I'd seen the letter. Maybe I did, though, and just forgot. I can't remember. Never mind.'

While his Mum was lost in thought, Jonny

began pushing Pete up the stairs, desperate to avoid any more questions from her.

'Oh well, this means there's plenty of room for your friend. You're welcome to stay, Pete.'

'This will be your room,' Jonny said, ignoring the sign on the door and showing Pete into Ted's bedroom.

Pete had a quick look round and then sat silently down on the bed.

'Did you see my list of likes on the Sibling Swap form?' Jonny asked.

Pete shook his head.

'So, I like riding my bike,' said Jonny. 'How about you?'

Pete shook his head quickly. 'Nope.'

'That's OK, because I also really like swimming ...'

Pete shook his head again. 'I don't.'

'Messing about?' tried Jonny.

'No!' said Pete.

'Doughnuts?'

'Yuck!' said Pete, pulling a face. 'I don't eat doughnuts.'

Odd, thought Jonny. *What kind of person doesn't eat doughnuts?*

'I also put down that I like computer games,' said Jonny.

At this, Pete looked up at Jonny and, finally, smiled.

'Do you have an Xbox?' Pete asked.

'Sure,' said Jonny. 'Shall we play for a bit? Then maybe we could take Widget to the Common or ...'

Pete had already pushed past Jonny and was on his way downstairs. Before Jonny even made it into the living room, he could hear the Xbox loading. Pete was staring intently at the screen. He didn't seem to notice that Widget was licking his face.

'Let's go, er, whoever you are,' said Pete. 'Two player!'

'It's Jonny ...' said Jonny. 'I'm your new brother.'

Pete said nothing. He was already shooting aliens. Jonny shrugged. Pete would learn his name soon, of course he would. In the meantime, there were aliens to take care of.

Jonny picked up his controller and the two new brothers began to play.

CHAPTER TWENTY-SIX

HOG IT

An hour later Jonny put his controller down and fell backwards on the rug.

'Wow, you're really good at this,' he said. 'Respect, brother!'

He held up his hand for a high five.

Pete carried on playing.

'Don't leave me hanging!' said Jonny.

Pete left him hanging.

'Ted never used to play the Xbox with me,' said Jonny. 'But then he used to moan that I hogged it and he couldn't get a go ...'

Pete didn't respond.

'Come and lay the table, please!' Jonny's mum shouted from the kitchen.

'Come on, we better go. Dinner's nearly ready,' said Jonny. 'See that zombie you're about to shoot? That's what my mum will look like if she has to call us in to dinner again!'

'I'm fine,' Pete said, eyes glued to the screen.

'But you must be hungry,' said Jonny.

'Not really,' said Pete.

He continued playing, without looking up. Jonny stood there for a moment, dithering and feeling rather abandoned by his new brother, and then ran into the kitchen. He had to fib that Pete didn't feel well, and he and his mum had dinner together, just the two of them. Then he ate an apple. Then he read his book. Then he learned his spellings for the test tomorrow. Then he helped his mum trim Widget's eyebrows. All the while, no sign of Pete.

Finally, as it was a lovely summer evening, Jonny asked Pete to come for a dog walk.

Pete didn't seem to hear. He was still glued to the Xbox, shoulders hunched.

'Come on!' Jonny exploded. 'Let's go! It's so boring you being on the Xbox all the time. Let's go out. Let's do something.'

'I need to finish this level,' said Pete.

Jonny sat down heavily on the sofa and sighed. Widget, with his lead on, sat down too. They waited. Then waited some more. And some more. At first, Pete had made Jonny feel a little anxious and shut out. Now, though, Pete's behaviour just made him angry.

'I give up!' he snapped. 'I'll take the dog out on my own.'

Jonny stomped off to the Common. He walked to the copse and found the place where he and Ted liked to build dens. It was just along from the Hanging Pants of Doom. He glanced at them, fluttering faintly in the evening breeze, and sighed.

When he got home Pete had gone to bed. He went to say goodnight and found him lying there, staring at the ceiling, his thumbs still twitching like they were working a controller.

'Night, then,' Jonny said.

Pete ignored him.

CHAPTER TWENTY-SEVEN

NIGHT FIGHT

That night, Jonny woke to the sound of gunfire. He sat up in bed, his heart pounding. **BOOM BOOM BOOM!** went the guns. **BOOM BOOM BOOM!** went Jonny's heart, perfectly in time.

Listening intently, he realised that it wasn't war outside, it was war inside, on the telly, in his living room. Pete! On the Xbox! At 1 a.m.?

Jonny tiptoed downstairs. He felt oddly excited. This was properly against-the-rules stuff. Playing Xbox at night! Pete was actually doing this! Unbelievable! Forbidden! Downright *naughty*!

Jonny peered into the living room. It was

dark except for the screen, which illuminated Pete's face with a ghostly light. His eyes looked slightly crazy as he worked the controller in his hands, taking out aliens.

BOOM BOOM BOOM!

'Holy cheese and pickle rolly,' whispered Jonny, crouching by his side and grabbing the TV remote. 'I can't believe you're doing this. Mum will go ballistic if she hears us. Just let me turn it down a bit.'

Pete didn't even look at him.

'Can I play too?' Jonny whispered.

'I'm in the middle of a level,' Pete grunted.

'OK, but give me a go in a minute,' said Jonny.

Fifteen minutes later he still hadn't had a go.

'Come on!' he said to Pete. 'Let's do two-player! You're hogging it. Hogger!'

Hogging it! Jonny remembered, with a jolt,

that 'hogging it' was what Ted accused him of doing with the Xbox. *Do I really hog it?* he wondered. *Hope not, because it's pretty frustrating when you are not the hogger but the one being hogged against.*

Eventually, Pete let Jonny join in, and the boys were consumed by the game, sitting in their pyjamas in the almost dark in the wee small hours. The pair carried on gaming like time meant nothing. Suddenly, it was 3 a.m. Time did mean something, after all. It meant that Jonny was tired. He yawned.

'Let's go back up, Pete, it's late,' he said.

Pete didn't seem to hear.

'You must need to sleep. You look super tired,' said Jonny.

Nothing from Pete, so Jonny reached over and flicked the TV off.

Pete just sat there, in the dark, his thumbs still working the controller.

'Come on,' whispered Jonny. 'Time for bed, let's go.'

'More!' said Pete. 'Play more.'

He flicked the TV back on. Jonny flicked it off. Pete flicked it back on. Jonny turned it off. On, off, on, off, faster and faster, each boy becoming more and more determined, until Widget, sensing the tension, began hopping about between the two of them, barking.

'Shush, Widge,' hissed Jonny. 'You'll wake Mum!'

Jonny shut Widget in the hallway and then went to take the controller from Pete. But Pete would not let it go.

What the heck was wrong with this guy? Jonny liked Xbox as much as the next nine-year-old, but at three in the morning? Come on! Jonny was tired. Wasn't Pete? And besides, Pete was the younger brother.

Shouldn't he listen to Jonny? Just like Jonny always did with Ted … Oh, yeah, that didn't always happen, true. But how about this, then? Pete was new here. He was new to the house. That meant he should do what Jonny said. End of.

Pete gripped the controller even tighter. Jonny held both hands up in a 'hey, relax' gesture. Then, remembering all those tense, stick-up situations in the adventure films he liked, where the hero used words not weapons to disarm a baddie, Jonny began to speak, clearly and calmly.

'It's my house, Pete, and I say it's time for bed,' said Jonny. 'Are you going to come quietly?'

'Never!' said Pete. He clutched the controller to his chest. 'You'll never take me upstairs! Never!'

'Drop the controller now, Pete,' said Jonny.

'Just put it down on the floor in front of you and everything will be fine.'

As Jonny talked he edged nearer to Pete.

'We do not have a problem here, Pete,' said Jonny. 'We're cool. It's all cool. It's just bedtime, that's all. But first, you need to hand me that controller, nice and easy now …'

But instead of passing it to him, Pete grabbed something from the floor and brandished it like a club. It was Widget's heavy rubber bone.

Jonny froze.

'Pete, I want you to drop your weapon!' he said, urgency in his voice now. 'Nobody needs to get hurt here.'

Jonny took another step towards Pete, who swung the bone madly at him.

'Drop your weapon. I repeat: DROP! YOUR! WEAPON!'

Pete swiped again.

'OK, this is officially a code red,' said Jonny. 'I'm calling for backup!'

He yanked the door open and Widget came bounding in.

'Disarm the assailant, Widge,' said Jonny.

Pete swung the bone at Widget in a 'keep back' kind of way, but all Widget saw was his favourite toy being waved in front of him and he did what any self-respecting dog would do – he grabbed it.

With the bone clamped in his jaws, a tug of war between Widget and Pete began. The two pulled and yanked and growled. Jonny spied his chance. He grabbed the games controller in Pete's other hand and began tugging too. Now Pete's arms were being pulled straight out from his body. He looked like a scarecrow with a dog attached to one hand and a boy to the other. The to-and-fro tugging proved too much.

Pete let go of the bone to concentrate on the controller. He clamped his free hand on it and with a giant, two-handed tug he ripped it from Jonny's grasp. Jonny crashed to the floor and watched Pete's hands jerk up and the controller fly out of them and straight through the window!

The **CRASH** was humungous, like a million greenhouses being dropped from a plane.

'You've broken the window!' gasped Jonny.

'Oh no no no NO!' gasped Pete, his hands to his face. 'Oh, Jonny, I'm so sorry. What have I done? I really didn't mean to break the window, I was just –'

'What on *earth*?' shouted Jonny's mum, rushing into the living room.

'It was completely and utterly my fault, Mrs Jonny. I'm just so terribly sorry,' spluttered Pete. 'What can I do to put this right?'

Jonny frowned. Not because of the window. Or his mum, furious in her nightie. But because of Pete, who sounded so sorry, so kind, so *nice*! This wasn't the monosyllabic, gruff, rude, computer-crazed geek Jonny had become used to. What was going on?

'Upstairs, both of you!' Jonny's mum said. 'I need to get this window boarded up right now, and you two need to go to bed, where you can't create any more mischief.'

There was no point protesting. Jonny led the way, but once inside Ted's bedroom he shut the door.

'I've had some fights with my real brother, Ted,' he hissed at Pete, 'but never anything like this.'

'I'm so sorry,' said Pete, looking like he might cry. 'I never meant for things to go this far. I can explain everything if you just give me a tiny-weensy chance ...'

'Explain?' said Jonny. 'No need. It's obvious: you're too crazy about Xbox.'

'I'm not really,' said Pete. 'That was all an act! I'm not any of those things. I'm not nine!

I'm twelve. My name's not Pete, it's Pip, and I'm not a boy, I'm really a girl. Sorry.'

Jonny gawped.

'The only thing that Sibling Swap got right about me is that I like computers,' said Pete-Pip. 'More than just Xbox, though. All sorts of programming and coding. I'm a bit of a tech whiz, really.'

'I don't understand,' spluttered Jonny.

'I noticed the Sibling Swap website when it first launched a few days back and it seemed like a cool idea, but I was curious about how it actually works,' she explained. 'I tried to find out a bit more about it, but I can't seem to track down who's behind it, although I think it must be local. So in the end I thought I'd trial it. I entered the wrong age and a false name and even lied about being a boy, but no one checked. Also, we don't have much in common, but the site still matched us up.

There are definitely some major issues with how it's set up and run.'

'I don't get it. What was with all the Xbox stuff?' Jonny asked, struggling to keep up.

'It was a disguise! A false identity! I thought I'd ham up the whole Xbox addiction thing, make myself really boring and unpleasant, to force you into swapping me. Then I could follow this through and see how the site responds,' said Pete-Pip.

'But why did you have to break my window?' Jonny huffed.

'I didn't mean to, of course! I'm really sorry about that,' said Pete-Pip. 'I was in character! But maybe that was taking it too far.'

'You could say that,' Jonny huffed again.

'I just wanted to test Sibling Swap in the field, you know?'

Jonny wasn't sure he did know.

'This is all so weird! *Too weird!* I don't want to hear anything else,' said Jonny. 'Just go to bed.'

'OK,' said Pete-Pip, 'but request a swap first.'

'But I don't know if I want another swap,' moaned Jonny, rubbing his tired eyes.

'Please, Jonny,' said Pete-Pip. 'Swap me back, so I can see what Sibling Swap does. I've come this far, I have to know how it ends!'

Pete-Pip smiled at him with her big brown eyes and then pulled up the Sibling Swap website on a little laptop she'd kept in her backpack. She passed it to Jonny. Mutely, he filled out a swap request form.

'Thank you,' said Pete-Pip. 'I'm sorry I wasn't straight with you, but I'm rather enjoying this spying lark. Sibling Swap is an interesting idea, isn't it?'

'I can't think about that right now,' said Jonny. 'I want to go to sleep. That's all. See you in the morning.'

Jonny didn't see Pete-Pip in the morning, though. She was gone before he woke up. And another brother was already heading his way.

CHAPTER TWENTY-EIGHT

D IS FOR DOUBT

Jonny felt tired and rather flat as he plodded into school that morning. The discovery that Pete was not even Pete but Pip, and that Sibling Swap seemed to send along pretty much anyone to be his brother was crushing his mood. What had happened to the massive database of possible matches that the site had banged on about? What about the dedicated team of Swap operatives who worked 24/7 to find the best match for you? Best match? What a joke. So far, all Jonny's brothers had been disasters in one way or another. Not a keeper among them. Perhaps Pete-Pip was right – the website was miles away from working smoothly!

Towards the end of the day Jonny had a new thought. It went like this:

Oh swear word.

He remembered there would probably be a new brother waiting for him when he got home, and rather than the usual flicker of excitement, he felt weary and a little nervous. He would have to get to know somebody new all over again and try to make being brothers work. This was starting to feel like eating soup with chopsticks – difficult and frustrating. None of the brothers Sibling Swap had sent him had worked out, despite Jonny's efforts. What if he got sent another non-perfect match? *Oh triple swear word with a big fat swear on top.*

Then Jonny had another thought. A thought that made him gasp like he'd seen a unicorn on a skateboard or found a duckling in his pocket. The thought was how nice it would be to go home and find ... not a new brother, but his original one: Ted. Not because Ted was great, but just because he knew what to expect with him. Ted would be slumped on the sofa, listening to a podcast. He would probably call Jonny a baby and send him out of the room. Jonny would probably blow him a raspberry and go get a biscuit. Simple! Jonny understood this kind of brother stuff. He'd been doing it all his life. It might not be fun or exciting, but it was familiar, comfy and predictable, like your favourite jumper. With these new siblings, though, he was navigating a whole new ocean of brotherly relations, without a map or compass or flask of reassuring hot chocolate.

Doubt was nibbling at his brain like a terrible zombie hamster of awfulness with very sharp teeth. By the time he began his walk home, Jonny had made up his mind.

Enough is enough, he thought. *I've had it. I'm done with sibling swapping for good. I don't care how fun this new brother seems or what he looks like, he's going back. This is over!*

As he walked up the front path, Jonny noticed the living-room window had been repaired. He stood in front of it. He could see his reflection. Then his reflection waved.

He leaped backwards in shock.

His reflection reappeared at the front door.

'Hello,' said Jonny to the reflection.

'Hi!' said the reflection.

The two boys stood in stunned silence for a few seconds, before Jonny blurted, 'Are we actually twins?'

'We are *so* similar!' said the boy.

And they were, right down to the same haircut and dark-brown eyes.

Then they burst out laughing – Jonny extra hard, because just a few seconds ago he was determined to send this brother back and put an end to sibling swapping. But now here he was, standing in front of a boy so similar to him, so exactly like him in every way, that he instantly forgot all that. Surely, *finally*, Sibling Swap had nailed it. Whoop! This had to be THE ONE!

'So what do you like?' Jonny asked as the two boys huddled around the kitchen table, eating Jaffa Cakes. 'I like biking, computer games –'

'Doughnuts and swimming!' said the new brother. 'I saw it all on the Sibling Swap form. That's exactly what I like too!'

'Cats or dogs?' Jonny asked.

'Dogs!' said the new brother.

'Pasta or potatoes?'

'Pasta!'

'Bath or shower?'

'Neither!'

'Correct!' said Jonny. 'You got all those right! We agree on everything. How about this – if you could have any super powers, what would they be?'

'First, magic,' said the new boy. 'Then, the power to go invisible. Third, the power to –'

'Melt marshmallows with laser beams that come out of your eyes?' said Jonny.

'EXACTLY!' shouted the boy. 'That's totally my third power!'

'Amazing!' said Jonny. 'You're just like me! We're so similar! Don't leave me hanging!'

The new brother high-fived him and the two boys grinned at each other.

'Oh heck, I don't even know your name!' Jonny blurted. 'Sorry!'

'Jonny,' said the boy.

'Yes?' said Jonny.

'No, my name is Jonny,' said the boy.

'Really?' said Jonny. 'Same as me?'

The other Jonny nodded.

'How's that going to work, then?'

'Brilliantly!' said the new brother. 'It means there's hardly anything to tell us apart. Not even our names! Imagine the adventures we can have if no one can spot the difference between us!'

'Twice the fun!' joked Jonny.

'Or double the trouble!' said his new brother, winking.

'Can I give you a nickname, though?' said Jonny. 'Just for us to use? How about J2, like Jonny number two?'

The front door opened and closed. Jonny's mum was home.

'I can't wait to introduce you to Mum,' said Jonny. 'When she sees how similar we are, it will blow her head off!'

CHAPTER TWENTY-NINE

DISAPPEAR HERE ...

Jonny went to greet his mum, but when he got to the kitchen J2 had disappeared.

'You look puzzled,' said his mum. 'Everything all right? Are you surprised that I managed to get that window fixed so quickly? It was expensive, by the way. How on earth did you break it? Really, Jonny, I expect better from you.'

She carried on lecturing him for a bit longer, but he hardly heard her. He was far too excited about J2's arrival. Just when he'd thought sibling swapping would never work and *could* never work, they'd sent him J2. Perfect! Now, where had he got to? Eventually, Jonny found him upstairs.

'Why did you run off?' he asked.

'Your mum can't see me,' said J2.

'Yes she can. She's got really good eyesight,' said Jonny.

'I mean, we can't *let* her see me,' said J2. 'Not if we're going to make the most of how similar we look.'

'Oh, I *see* ...' said Jonny. 'You mean make the most of the whole lookie-likie thing? Trick people? Who's who? You're me and I'm you but no one else realises. That kind of thing ...'

J2 nodded.

'Jonny!' his mum called up the stairs. 'Can you run round to Charlie's shop and get some more milk?'

'I'll go,' J2 whispered. 'It will be a chance to see if other people think I'm you.'

Jonny felt a shiver of excitement. 'OK, let's try it!' he said, giving him directions.

'The whole mission should take no more than five minutes. Good luck!'

Jonny waited nervously while J2 headed round to the shop. He watched the clock. Five minutes became six.

It's taking too long. Something's gone wrong. Something's up, he thought. *Please say Charlie hasn't guessed that J2 isn't me. What if he has? What if he knows J2 is trying to trick him and he's cross, so he's put him in the fizzy-drink fridge? But wait! Charlie would never do that, he's too nice. Or maybe he's called in Mrs Algernon to quiz J2 with her scary, serious face and those eyes … Maybe Fat Stanley is sitting on J2's chest, pinning him to the floor, so he can't escape while he's being questioned. Maybe …*

Then suddenly, silently, J2 appeared in his room, holding up the milk like a trophy!

'You did it!' shouted Jonny. 'Did Charlie guess?'

'No! He didn't have a clue that I'm not you! We even had a chat about school. He *seriously* thought I was you.'

'Amazing!' said Jonny. He dashed downstairs to deliver the milk, and when he returned to his room, J2 was sitting at his desk, making notes and drawing graphs.

'Think of the potential, Jonny,' said J2. 'If I can pass for you, we can share everything.

One of us can go to school while the other one stays home. If you don't like what's for dinner but I do, I can eat it instead. We can take it in turns to unload the dishwasher. Think of that! Half the chores! And no one will ever know!'

Jonny nodded, excited but slightly dazed.

'It's going to be amazing!' J2 continued. 'Now – fancy a day off school tomorrow? Do you? Well, allow me to take your place!'

CHAPTER THIRTY

BACKGROUND CHECKS

'OK, fill me in on your friends,' said J2, gripping a pencil, ready to take notes. So Jonny explained how George was his best mate and was mad about computers and coding. How his friend Alex always wore shorts, even if it was freezing out, and how Mya wanted to be a film director and had a collection of pine cones.

'And what about your family?' J2 asked, still scribbling madly. 'I need some background so I can be convincing.'

So Jonny told J2 how his parents had split up when he was seven, and his dad lived quite far away. How Jonny had been upset by his parents' divorce, and for almost a year afterwards he would creep into Ted's bed and sleep with him at night. How he and Ted used to build dens together out of the clothes airer and some blankets and old towels and pegs, and hide in there for ages with torches, telling each other stories. How Ted loved to eat chocolate spread and peanut butter sandwiches. How lately, since Ted was nearly a teenager, he didn't want to play and told Jonny to keep out of his room. How Ted always teased him about touching the Hanging Pants of Doom, and said Jonny hogged the Xbox and was rubbish at climbing. He said Ted was more boring these days, and that he missed how things used to be.

J2 wasn't writing a lot of this down. 'He must be a cool guy, though,' he said.

'Why?' Jonny asked.

'He was at the Sibling Swap warehouse when I was there. I never actually saw him, but his picture was up on the Star Swaps noticeboard. He was rated a Premium Swap. That's, like, the best!'

'Premium Swap?' Jonny spluttered.

'Yes, one of the best brothers on their books, so they were waiting to find the perfect home for him.'

Jonny looked astonished at this. 'What's so premium about Ted?'

'I dunno,' shrugged J2, 'but there was some blurb below his pic describing him. How he was mature and sensible, perfect older-brother material. Did his share of jobs around the house, like emptying the dishwasher and –'

'*I* empty the dishwasher!' shouted Jonny. 'It's not just Ted. He always goes on about how Mum lets me off stuff like hanging up the washing or emptying the dishwasher when I totally flipping swear word do it. Sometimes. Well, occasionally. Now and then, but I *do* do it!'

'Calm down! It's OK!' said J2. 'Come on, let's do some building with those bricks over there. Or draw moustaches on people in the newspaper. Or flick through some comics. I know you like to do all those things. You must do, because I do too.'

J2 was right. Jonny liked to do all those things.

The two boys spent a couple of happy hours together, only interrupted when Jonny went down for dinner. He managed to sneak some food up to J2, and by 9 p.m. the brothers were tired. J2 decided to sleep under Jonny's bed, out of the way, but, tucked in above him, Jonny couldn't doze off. He was thinking about Ted being rated a Premium Swap. Ha! What rubbish! No wonder Sibling Swap had sent him so many unsuitable brothers if they went around grading Ted as Premium. They obviously had no idea. Then Jonny realised something else was nagging at his brain. It wasn't the zombie hamster of doubt again, but it might have been its cousin, the nervous chipmunk of worry. Jonny remembered J2's plan to go into school the next day. It was certainly plucky! *But, oh swear word!* Jonny thought, with a gulp. *Was it also stupid? Dangerous even?*

'I've got an idea,' he whispered to J2. 'Why don't we just be brothers, like normal? Not pretending to actually be each other, you know?'

'No way!' whispered J2. 'This is going to be great.'

'OK, I suppose so,' said Jonny.

'I know so!' said J2. 'Us being identical is going to be the biggest adventure ever.'

Just a few days ago Jonny would have agreed, but now, after a hectic few days with Sibling Swap, he wasn't quite so sure ...

Jonny woke up feeling more positive, and was excited when J2 went off to school, looking freakishly, weirdly like Jonny. Once his mum had gone to work, Jonny emerged from his room and settled himself in front of the TV with a huge bowl of snacks and a can of Pixie Fizz. He passed several happy hours watching and munching, and even found time for a nap. When J2 finally came home, Jonny was still in his PJs.

'How was it?' Jonny asked. 'Did anybody guess? What did Mrs Flannery say? What about George? He's really clever. Did he spot anything?'

Slowly, the two boys unpicked the day, with J2 explaining how it went, who said what and where and when.

'It really worked,' said J2, grinning. 'That's what I'm telling you! Nobody guessed. They all think I'm you! So you know what this means? It's not like I'm your friend or just your brother. It's like I *am* you! The same person!'

'Amazing! I can't believe no one guessed,' Jonny said. 'I mean, thanks, guys. I thought you were my friends. No, just kidding, J2. It's cool, it's really great.'

'Great?' said J2, bubbling with excitement. 'This is more than great. This is big! Can't you see? This is huge! This is … epic!'

CHAPTER THIRTY-ONE

DOUBLE TROUBLE

This is not so epic, Jonny thought the next day, as he clung on to the shed in his garden, trying to prevent J2 from jumping off its roof. *This is a disaster.*

Let's rewind.

Jonny had gone to school in the morning as usual, his PE kit and bag slung over his shoulder, and J2 promised to stay at home watching telly all day, just as Jonny had the day before. Near the school gates he caught up with his friends, Mya and Alex.

'Morning!' Jonny said. 'Alex, why are you dressed as a fairy?'

'You told me it was Dress as a Fairy Day today!' said Alex.

'I didn't tell you anything!' said Jonny.

'You did, yesterday, at the end of school!' said Alex. 'My mum was up till midnight making this costume! Why is no one else wearing a fairy suit?'

'Oh, by the way,' said Mya, 'this is from my dad.' She passed Jonny a £10 note.

'He's really impressed by you raising funds to keep the teaspoon museum open in your gran's village. Says he'd like to help.'

'Teaspoon museum?' Jonny spluttered. 'I've never heard of a teaspoon museum in my gran's village. My gran lives in a town, anyway ...'

'Really?' said Mya, a grin bursting across her face. She snatched the £10 back. 'Great! I'll be having this, then!'

The bell went just as George ran into the playground. The two friends sat at their table in the classroom and Jonny got his pencil case out of his backpack. Inside, every pencil was chewed and every pen lid was chomped and mangled. Yuck!

'Think that might have happened yesterday,' whispered George. 'You seemed a tiny bit more nervous than usual.'

'Me? I wasn't nervous. I wasn't even ...' Jonny trailed off. He wasn't even in school, was he? And George seemed to know it. He raised his eyebrows.

'It's OK, I get it,' George whispered, and then winked. 'You weren't here, were you, Jonny? It was your new, almost identical brother, wasn't it? Don't worry, no one else guessed. No one except me. I knew, of course.'

'You did?' Jonny asked. 'How?'

'Well, you know, because I'm your best friend,' said George. 'It's my job to know.'

When it was time for PE, Jonny pulled his kit from his bag. Only it wasn't his kit. It was his panda onesie. The teacher made him wear it for rounders, all the same. His friends laughed and Jonny felt stupid. And also hot. Doing rounders in a panda onesie doesn't work. As the class got changed, George explained how Jonny's new lookie-likie brother had tried to climb a tree while wearing the PE kit, but was so hopeless at climbing that he'd got stuck hanging on a branch and had ripped the shorts and T-shirt.

'He must have panicked and shoved the onesie in as a replacement for the ruined kit,' said George.

Maybe, thought Jonny. And at the end of the day he raced home to find out. All these tales of fairy days and teaspoon museums, all this pencil-noshing and PE kit mucking-upness was the fault of one person.

'J2!' Jonny shouted as soon as he got home. 'Why have you been telling fibs to my friends and messing about with my PE kit? And ...'

J2 appeared at the top of the stairs, smiling.

'I can explain!' he said. 'There were maybe one or two small issues yesterday which I maybe didn't quite tell you about. The pencil-chewing ... well, I was just a bit nervous! And the fairy day was just a joke. I didn't think Alex would take it seriously.'

'Well, Alex doesn't have a great sense of humour,' said Jonny.

'What about the onesie?' Jonny asked. 'Mrs Flannery made me wear that for PE, and I was roasting!'

'I ripped your PE kit,' J2 said. 'Sorry! I was trying to climb a tree. Showing off, I suppose. I wanted to impress your friends!'

'But they're supposed to be *your* friends already – no need to impress them. You're supposed to be me, after all.'

'Sorry,' said J2. 'I won't be so nervous when I go in tomorrow. I can pull off this being you act, I know I can.'

'I don't know if you *should* go in as me tomorrow!' said Jonny.

J2 looked a bit worried but didn't say anything.

'Well, let's forget about it all for now,' said Jonny. 'How about I go to Charlie's shop to get some sweets?'

'Or we could just have a biscuit from the cupboard?' said J2, looking … What was it? Guilty? Nervous? Jonny wasn't quite sure. He ignored it and shook out his piggy bank and then ran off down the stairs, dreaming of bonbons.

CHAPTER THIRTY-TWO

NAME AND BLAME

'How dare you show your face in here again!' Charlie shouted when Jonny stepped inside the corner shop.

Jonny froze. Charlie was nice, normally. He was friendly and helpful, normally. He never, ever yelled, normally.

'Get out, thief!' shouted Charlie, running towards him.

Jonny tore out of the shop, his mind a swirly whirl of confusion, his hair in his eyes and then ...

CRASH!

He ran straight into Mrs Algernon.

'Stop right there!' she boomed. 'I want to speak with you!'

She looked even meaner than usual. *Oh stuffed-crust misery!* thought Jonny. *They're all out to get me!*

'You deliberately let your dog off the lead today when you could see my cat was out on the front step,' she growled.

Jonny had no idea what Mrs Algernon was on about. Cat? Front step? Today? Eh?

Charlie had caught up with him now.

'He stole from my shop earlier,' puffed Charlie. 'A sherbet fountain and a couple of those curly sweets.'

'Frizzy Pops?' asked Mrs Algernon.

'No, not them,' said Charlie.

'Corkscrew Curlers?' suggested Mrs Algernon.

'No,' said Charlie.

'Honeycomb Helix? Insanity Spirals? Midget Twists? Tupenny Twine Bars? Mint Crimps?'

'Mint Crimps!' said Charlie. 'That's them!'

'Oh dear,' said Mrs Algernon. 'You should *never, ever* steal Mint Crimps.'

'But I was in school all day,' Jonny protested.

'No, you weren't,' said both the adults.

'With my own eyes, I saw you walk into my shop, help yourself to my sweets and leg it,' said Charlie. 'Are you calling my own eyes liars?'

Jonny wasn't doing that, no.

'Your dog had my cat pinned down,' said Mrs Algernon. 'If I hadn't given him a smart kick up the necessaries, he might have killed poor Stanley.'

Widget loathed Fat Stanley, and Jonny could easily believe that he would want to pin him down, but that wasn't the point. The point was that none of this was Jonny. He had not been involved in any of this nicking and narkery.

'It must have been someone who looks like me,' said Jonny, guessing who was to blame here. This just made the two grown-ups do a sort of 'don't give me that' laugh.

'We know what you look like, young man,' said Mrs Algernon. 'We wouldn't be fooled by anyone else.'

'What's going on?' asked Jonny's mum, arriving at the scene on her way home from work.

'He's been stealing and allowing his dog to menace my cat,' said Mrs Algernon.

'He called my eyes liars!' said Charlie.

'Really?' she said. She looked at Jonny and then back at Charlie and Mrs Algernon.

'Thank you,' she said. 'Leave this with me. I'd like to speak to my son in private if you don't mind.'

The two angry adults looked like they did mind, actually, but they stood aside as Jonny's mum led him back to the house.

CHAPTER THIRTY-THREE

IDENTITY CRISIS

In the kitchen Jonny's mum quizzed him about the stealing and cat crushing. Jonny denied both. Then Widget came into the room. He was walking a bit funny, presumably thanks to Mrs Algernon's size-seven foot making contact with his bottom earlier that day.

Jonny's mum raised her eyebrows and pointed at the limping dog. Jonny still denied everything, begging her to ring the school if she didn't believe him.

When she got through to his teacher she confirmed that, yes, Jonny had been in school all day, although he'd lost a house point for bringing a panda onesie instead of his PE kit.

'So, what on earth has been going on?' Jonny's mum asked him. 'What are Charlie and Mrs Algernon talking about?'

'Don't know. They've gone mad or blind or both or something,' said Jonny, getting up and edging towards the door. 'Bye!'

Jonny charged upstairs. Where was J2? Where was that little lookie-likie brother? *Terrible twin more like*, thought Jonny, as he threw his bedroom door open.

'You just got me in another huge stinking pile of trouble,' he fumed when he found J2 in his room. 'Nicking sweets – what the flipping hecksters?'

'I panicked,' said J2. 'I'm sorry. Being you was a tiny bit scarier than I'd guessed it might be. I suddenly thought Charlie had worked out that I wasn't really you, so I freaked and ran out of the shop.'

'Well, he hadn't guessed!' said Jonny.

'Which is why I'm for it! They definitely do think you're me! They don't realise you're not me, that you're someone else who just looks like me and that only me is actually me!'

J2 smiled nervously.

'What about Widget attacking Fat Stanley?' Jonny asked. 'Did you panic then too?'

'Widget just pulled and got away,' said J2. 'I didn't know he had it in for that cat. You didn't tell me.'

'I couldn't tell you everything!' said Jonny. 'If you were my real brother you'd have known.'

'Well, you swapped your real brother,' said J2, getting cross now. 'So it's your stupid fault. If you want someone who knows everything your real brother knows, then you should have just kept your real brother!'

J2 had rather hit the nail on the head there. Swapping Ted had seemed like a beautifully simple idea. How wrong Jonny had been!

'I thought a new brother would be better,' Jonny wailed. 'You must have done too, otherwise why did you put yourself up for a swap?'

'I didn't!' shrieked J2, with an outraged face. 'My brother Fred did. He asked for a new sibling. Just like you did with Ted. I didn't ask to be swapped!'

Jonny felt a wave of guilt crash over him. He'd been thinking so much about finding a new brother, he hadn't properly considered how it felt for Ted, or for all the brothers he kept rejecting. J2 was upset, but what about Mervyn, Hari, Henry, Alfie and Pete?

'One minute I'm minding my own business,' J2 continued, 'next minute I'm in a big warehouse which smells of fish! Then I'm told to wait there until they find me a suitable swap.'

'That's where you saw Ted's picture?' Jonny asked. 'Was he there too?'

'Probably,' said J2. 'I was shut in a little room. I didn't see anyone, then I was sent here. When I saw how similar we were I thought, OK, maybe this will be good, maybe this could actually be fun. I was trying to make it work. But I was wrong.'

The two boys were quiet for a few seconds.

'So what are you going to do now?' Jonny asked.

'Not sure,' J2 said. He looked a bit tearful. 'You don't want me, and neither does my real brother! I guess I'll go back to the Sibling Swap warehouse and see if they can help me.'

J2 pushed past him and ran downstairs.

'Wait!' said Jonny, running after him. 'Let me put things right!'

J2 had run outside and was climbing up the shed at the end of the garden, preparing to leap down on to the path beyond and leg it.

'Stop! Please!' yelled Jonny. 'Don't go!'

He felt as though his life was spinning out of control. All these brothers. All this failure. Ted gone. Hurt feelings all round. 'Please come down!' he moaned. But J2 didn't budge, so Jonny upturned a bucket, stood on it and tried to grab J2's trouser leg to stop him jumping off.

'Get off!' said J2, kicking him away. Jonny lunged and grasped the other trouser leg, and again J2 kicked him off. On and on this went. Lunge, grab, kick, lunge, grab, kick. It looked like J2 was doing a little jig up there on the roof. Finally, he edged to the far end, preparing to leap to freedom. Jonny put his foot on the shed's door handle and pushed up a little higher.

'Let's sort this out together,' he gasped, gripping the shed roof with his fingernails. 'Like brothers!'

'But I'm not your brother,' said J2. 'Ted is.'

With that, J2 jumped off and ran away.

Jonny was left flattened to the side of the shed, clinging to its rough surface.

Ted is my brother, he thought. *Only Ted.* And on that bombshell, the door handle his foot was resting on gave way.

CHAPTER
THIRTY-FOUR

WHO'S BEEN SLEEPING IN MY SHED?

CRASH!

Jonny's foot smashed through the door, which swung open violently. His nails left claw marks on the edge of the shed roof as he tried to cling on, before he landed on his back inside the shed, with one foot still stuck in the door.

'Welcome!' said a voice.

Jonny looked up and yelped like he'd seen a ghost. Only he hadn't seen a ghost. Not this time.

'Pete?' said Jonny.

'Pip, actually. Remember?' she said. 'Or Pete-Pip. That's fine if it's easier. Whatever you like. Anyway! Good to see you! Do you want some help getting your foot out of the door?'

Pete-Pip was sitting at a desk that almost filled the shed. It was loaded with tech, including a laptop, several monitors and three separate keyboards.

'Where have you … ? How did you … ? Eh … ?!' Jonny spluttered. 'Didn't you go back to Sibling Swap?'

'Umm, no, in the end, I didn't!' said Pete-Pip. 'I was going to, then I realised I might be better off observing your next swap, rather than being one myself. Then I noticed your shed and got set up here! Thanks for the Wi-Fi, by the way. Here, let's get your leg free.'

'So are you going home?' Jonny asked, sitting down now that his foot was liberated from the shed door.

'Soon,' said Pete-Pip. 'I wanted to complete my research and see how your next brother panned out.'

'Oh, thanks,' he said. Jonny thought that was quite nice of Pete-Pip, although he didn't like to admit it out loud.

'Will you be getting another swap now that the other guy has gone?' Pete-Pip asked, pointing at the shed roof.

J2! Jonny had momentarily forgotten

about him. Then he shuddered, as if shaking off a bad dream.

'Another swap?' he said. 'No. There won't be another swap. This is over. Sibling Swap is over! Flipping swear word, it's all over, over, over! It doesn't work, and I want out. I don't want any new brothers or ghost brothers or meerkat brothers or merboys or little crazy betting kids or a tech-mad brother who isn't even a brother, he's a sister or ...'

'What *do* you want, then?' asked Pete-Pip.

Jonny blinked hard and thought for a second.

'I want my real brother back,' he said. 'I want Ted.'

CHAPTER THIRTY-FIVE

OH SWEAR WORD!

'I want Ted.'

What a difference three words make! Suddenly, Jonny knew. He knew it all. He had finally realised that you can't simply trade in your brother because he teases you or laughs at your climbing skills or gives you wedgies. You can't swap your brother just because he's older and bigger and sometimes bosses you around. It was all glaringly, painfully clear now. Jonny understood, but it all felt a bit late.

'Good idea!' said Pete-Pip. 'Just log on to Sibling Swap and ask for him back. Here ...'

She passed a laptop to Jonny. He logged on with shaking fingers and hit the

'REQUEST A RETURN' button. He suddenly felt excited. OK, he hadn't worked out what he would say to Ted when he came home, but he knew now, very clearly, that he had to get him back.

A message flashed up in red.

SITE UNDER CONSTRUCTION – ACTION DENIED

'What does that mean? Site under construction? No!' gasped Jonny, clicking on the 'REQUEST A RETURN' button again and again. Each time, an 'ACTION DENIED' message appeared, accompanied by a depressing **thunk** sound. The sound of failure.

Jonny stared at the screen in panic, then spotted a line of explanation at the bottom.

DUE TO MASSIVE LEVELS OF DEMAND, SIBLING SWAP IS BEING RESTRUCTURED AND HAS CLOSED UNTIL FURTHER NOTICE. WE WILL RELAUNCH AGAIN VERY SOON.

That was it? The whole website had been shut down? Just like that? For 'restructuring', whatever that meant.

Oh, mega-droppings times five thousand. There was only one thing to do …

Jonny collapsed on to the shed floor and howled. What a mess! What a stinking, rubbish, ploppy mess! Thanks to Sibling Swap, his mum had been scared out of her wits, his neighbours had been upset and his dog had been kicked up the bottom. A whole bunch of possible brothers had been messed about too, and were now – what? – stranded in some warehouse who knew where. Worst of all, Jonny had lost Ted. His actual brother. What a miserable, horrible, stupid disaster!

'I'll never see him again,' wailed Jonny. 'I've ruined everything. Ted! Where are you? I'm sorry. I'm so sorry! What have I done? What have I done? What have I –'

'Made a fool and a ninny of yourself, that's what, my lad,' came a deep voice. 'Now stand up and let's make amends.'

'Your Brilliantness!' gasped Jonny. He scrambled to his feet, sniffing.

'I could hear your bleating all the way over on the Other Side,' said Henry. 'What a carry on! Now, you wish to have your real brother back?'

'Yes, but the computer says Sibling Swap has closed down,' Jonny wailed. 'I've lost Ted! I've ruined everything! I've –'

'Nonsense!' said Henry firmly. 'You only swapped him. You didn't chop off his head. There's a big difference. Trust me, I know. Of course you can get him back.'

'How?' sniffed Jonny. 'I don't know how to find him!'

'Use your friends,' said Henry. 'Gather your best people around you. That's what I did. Do you think I ruled England alone? I had help, you know. You need loyal supporters, men you can trust as though they were your brothers!'

'Umm, sorry to interrupt, but who are you talking to?' whispered Pete-Pip, looking around the shed.

'It's the ghost of Henry the Eighth, you just can't see him,' said Jonny. 'I can though. We were brothers for a bit.'

Then Jonny blew his nose and took a deep breath.

'Henry, you say I need loyal supporters?'

Henry nodded.

'Well, since Ted left I've had quite a few brothers,' said Jonny. 'Two of you are right here, and that's a start. Will you be my band of brothers?'

Pete-Pip and Henry nodded solemnly.

'Did he agree?' whispered Pete-Pip. 'I still can't see him.'

'Yeah, he nodded,' said Jonny, then he puffed out a huge breath and looked serious.

'OK,' he said. 'Let's get to work!'

CHAPTER THIRTY-SIX

TRACKING TED

'First, we need to work out where Sibling Swap is,' said Jonny. 'J2 said it was a warehouse or something, and Alfie said it was on the edge of town. Did you ever go there?'

'No,' said Pete-Pip. 'I was sent straight here. I've already tried to trace the site headquarters, but there's nothing, which is really peculiar. No address, the website isn't registered anywhere, no contact details. It's ever so odd. But let's have a look around town for anything that fits the bill.'

Pete-Pip then hacked into some of the town's CCTV cameras, bringing up images of shopping centres and the ring road, and then ...

'What about this?' she said. The screen showed an industrial estate.

'Could be that,' said Jonny. 'There are quite a few warehouses there, though. We'll have to check them all out.'

'The place is only about a mile from here,' said Pete-Pip. 'You better get going. I'll keep an eye on the CCTV for anything suspicious.'

'This is it, then!' said Jonny. 'Pete, I mean Pip, I mean Pete-Pip, call me if you spot anything. Henry, come with me. I might need some regal muscle. We need to find Ted and bring him home, and we need to do it *right now*.'

CHAPTER THIRTY-SEVEN

WHAT'S IN THE WAREHOUSE?

Twenty minutes later the pair were standing on the edge of the industrial estate. There were four warehouses scattered across weedy concrete.

'I'll start with that one,' said Jonny, pointing at the nearest. 'Henry, you case out the one next to it.'

Jonny pushed open the doors of the first warehouse and saw a security guard dozing by the front desk. A strong smell hit him. What was it? Dog food? Then he saw a sign. Premier Pies. This couldn't be the right place. He ducked back outside and saw Henry wafting towards him, shaking his head.

'Some sort of cabinetmakers,' said Henry. 'Nary a child in there – I checked everywhere.'

'Let's try over here,' said Jonny, and sprinted off towards the furthest warehouse.

Inside, an unmistakable smell of fish hit Jonny's nostrils. Henry spluttered a bit and curled his lip.

'By the mass, what a stench! I'm more of a mutton man, myself,' he said. 'I'll investigate outside.'

Jonny pushed through a door and into an area full of huge freezers. It was cold and smelly. No sign of any children. He tiptoed forward and pulled open the heavy door of one of the freezers. Fish fingers! Thousands of them, stacked up like breaded bars of gold. But that wasn't all. Looking around the room Jonny saw towers of boxes piled in one corner. One contained flashing budgie collars,

'So you can always spot your bird in the dark!', and another was bursting with sachets of dehydrated shepherd's pie. There was a sack full of battery-powered eye massagers and a couple of plastic trays with boxes of chocolate-coated sprouts, 'A taste sensation'. What was all this stuff, and who would keep it here? The fish fingers, all these weird gadgets and gear: they all made a bell ring in Jonny's head, but it was muffled, like the bell was inside a sock or under a bear.

Then Jonny noticed another door and pushed it open. It was warmer on the other side, and less pongy. There were several long rows of cubicles, similar to the ones in the changing rooms at a swimming pool. Jonny tried the door of one. Locked! He tried another and another. All locked!

'Hello?' he whispered. 'Anyone here?'

'Hello?' 'Hello?' 'Hi, hello?' Several voices

answered Jonny – voices coming from inside the cubicles. How many children were in here, all locked up and waiting to be swapped? Then Jonny heard a voice he recognised.

'Jonny!' A tiny blond boy jumped up and down in a cubicle a little way off. 'I told you I could run down here in ten minutes. We had a bet, remember? And I won. Obviously!'

Alfie!

Jonny ran to Alfie's cubicle.

'Never mind about the bet. I can help you, but first I have to find Ted. Where is he?' Jonny shouted through the door.

'He was in the next room to me,' said Alfie. 'He's really extra upset, Jonny! He says he's never going home again, not after how you treated him.'

At this, Jonny felt sick. He rattled the door of the next cubicle.

'Ted! Ted! Are you in there?'

No answer.

'Don't bother,' said Alfie. 'He said that as you don't want him, he's off.'

'No!' said Jonny, rattling the door again. Then he heard a squeak from the next cubicle over and the sound of digging.

'Hari?' he said.

A squeak came back in reply. Yes! Jonny grabbed a box, hopped up on to it and looked into Hari's cubicle.

'Oh my pancakes!' he muttered.

The floor of Hari's cubicle wasn't a floor any more. It was a building site. There were piles of earth everywhere and, heading down into what had been Ted's room, a tunnel. A very definite tunnel.

Jonny hurriedly moved the box and squinted into what had been Ted's space. There was another tunnel opening here, and it led, most definitely, through the wall and out of the warehouse.

'Oh Satan's sausages!' muttered Jonny, fearing the worst. He ran out, past the freezers, out of the front door and around the side of the warehouse. There was Hari, still working on his tunnel.

'Hari!' Jonny spluttered. 'What have you done? The tunnel! Did you let Ted escape?'

SQUEAK. Yes!

'Noooo,' said Jonny, his hands thrust into his hair, his face a picture of despair. 'Where did he go?'

But Hari was too busy scuffling around in his beautiful meerkat tunnel to listen.

'What's this?' boomed Henry, ghosting alongside Jonny and spotting Hari's masterpiece.

'Ted's escaped,' Jonny explained to Henry, trying to keep his voice from sounding panicked. 'Hari dug a tunnel and Ted used it to get out.'

'The fool!' said Henry, glowering at Hari.

'It's not his fault. He's a meerkat, sort of. Digging's what they do,' said Jonny. 'We have to find Ted, though. Maybe he's at home? Please be at home!'

He rang Pete-Pip, explaining that Ted had escaped and asking if he had showed up at home. No. Pete-Pip offered to send her drone out to look for him.

'You have a drone?' Jonny asked.

'Of course,' said Pete-Pip. 'I have several!'

Wow, she was good! Having a computer-geek girl ex-brother living in your shed certainly had its benefits.

'He's not at home,' said Jonny, turning to Henry. 'We have to find him. He's angry with me and thinks I don't want him, so he's run away. Where is he? We have to track him down before he gets too far and disappears for good.'

'What about me?' shouted Alfie. He was

peeping through a window, watching the whole scene.

'I'll come back for you, Alfie, I promise!' shouted Jonny, waving at his little ex-brother, whose blond hair shone brightly, even through the grubby window. 'But first I have to find Ted.'

With that, Jonny began running, with Hari bounding along behind him.

'Huzzah!' cried Henry. 'The hunt is on!'

CHAPTER THIRTY-EIGHT

REUNITED! AND IT FEELS SO BAD ...

Almost immediately, Hari stopped and barked twice. Danger!

A slightly overweight guard dog around the back of the warehouse was barking and snapping madly. Jonny noticed that the rope tying him up looked horribly flimsy, but, luckily, Henry had a plan.

'Silence, cur!' said Henry, lobbing a yoghurt towards the dog. Instantly, it stopped barking and began licking it up.

'Awesome!' said Jonny.

'I always keep a few yoghurts down my codpiece in case I get peckish. I suppose you could call it a yog-piece!' said Henry, guffawing and slapping his thigh. At least someone was having a good time.

Jonny was thinking and running, thinking and running, thinking and …

'I've got it!' he shouted, stopping dead. 'I know where Ted is. He has to be at the Common. It's obvious, of course. Yes, yes, yes, yes, yes! It's our favourite place, where we always made dens. There's even a sealed box buried in a hidden hole we dug, and it's got snacks and water in it. He'd go there first to grab supplies before heading away. Wouldn't he? Oh, please say he would! We have to try there, anyway. Come on! This way!'

Quickly, he called Pete-Pip and asked her to head over there with her drone. Ten minutes of rapid sprinting later, with Jonny chanting, 'Please be there, please be there,' under his breath the whole way, and the brothers arrived at the Common.

'Ah, this excellent place,' said Henry. 'I like it well. Fine hunting country. Pity we don't have the hounds with us. They could find your brother in no time.'

'No need. I know where he'll be,' said Jonny, pointing at a copse in the distance. 'There, for sure. Has to be. It's our secret hideout, not far from the Hanging Pants of Doom tree, remember?'

Pete-Pip appeared, puffing from her run, the drone buzzing overhead.

'You can bring your drone down,' Jonny said. 'I know where Ted is.'

The band of brothers headed into the copse. They arrived at the den site, but where was Ted? Had he left already? Was Jonny just plain wrong about him coming here? Then goosebumps prickled on his arms. It was the same feeling he'd had when Henry appeared in his bedroom. That sense of being watched.

Someone was staring at Jonny, silently. All of a sudden he understood. Ted was an excellent climber. He wouldn't be on the ground, he would go ...

'Up there!' shouted Jonny, looking up to see his brother standing on a branch. 'Ted! Ted! You're here! I found you!' he spluttered, hopping up and down with excitement, but then Ted spoke.

'Who are *you*?' he said.

'It's me!' said Jonny. 'It's Jonny, your brother. Come to say sorry and take you home. Sorry. There, I've said it. Now let's go home!'

'But that's my brother, there,' he said.

J2 was shimmying round the tree trunk, a few branches below Ted.

'What? That's J2!' shouted Jonny, almost laughing. 'Not me! *I'm* me, of course.'

J2 shook his head. 'Who are you?' he asked.

'I've never met you before in my life. I'm Jonny and this is my brother, Ted.'

'That's right,' said Ted. 'We're brothers. And we don't know who you are, or any of these people with you.' He waved his hand dismissively at Pete-Pip and Hari.

'No, no, no, no, NO!' Jonny shouted up at the two boys. He pointed at J2. 'Forget about him, Ted. I'm Jonny! I'm the one. The original and proper brother. He just looks like me. I know you totally and utterly! I know how you always put the peanut butter on first when you're making a peanut butter and chocolate spread sandwich. I know you got car sick when you were eight and threw up in a bag of cheese puffs; that you had to go to A&E because you got your hand stuck in a jar; that your nickname for Widget is Sir Widgington McWidge of Widgeshire. I know you always go to sleep on your stomach;

that you're scared of woodlice; that your favourite sweets are Noshums; and you have a lucky key ring and ...'

Jonny looked like he might collapse. He was red in the face, panting and close to tears.

Ted looked at J2. 'What shall we do?' he whispered.

Jonny was staring up at them and whimpering, 'I know you're my brother, I know you're my brother ...'

'Maybe we need to stop?' said J2 quietly, looking down at Jonny, who was wringing his hands and then pulling at his hair.

Ted nodded and shouted, 'OK, that's enough. I get it. You're Jonny. Calm down with the whining!'

'Oh, thank Tuesdays!' said Jonny, doing a giddy little twirl of relief. 'I'm Jonny. I'm Jonny. One hundred per cent your brother!

Thank you! Thank you! I promise I'm really your brother!'

'OK! I know!' said Ted. 'Actually, I knew all along.'

Jonny stopped dead, shocked. 'What?' he spluttered.

'I knew you were you, I just wasn't ready to come home, that's all,' explained Ted.

'I was feeling pretty hurt and didn't want to go home either,' said J2. 'Ted was just escaping through Hari's tunnel when I arrived at the warehouse, so we buddied up.'

'That's right,' said Ted. 'I was impressed by how like you J2 was, but I knew right away he wasn't *actually* you. I'd know you anywhere, Jonny. You're my brother. Plus, J2 doesn't run like you.'

'How do *I* run?' asked Jonny.

'Like you need the loo,' said Ted. 'It's a bit jerky, and you lean forwards.'

'I do not!' said Jonny, then he shook his head. 'Anyway, that isn't the point. The point is, I know I shouldn't have swapped you. I realise that now. It's clear as my own trousers. I utterly, utterly promise I won't do anything like this again. I'm sorry. Swapping you was totally stupid and was never going to work, really, thinking about it, but I've learned my lesson.'

'What lesson?' asked Ted.

'That we are brothers, for better or worse,' said Jonny. 'Even if I annoy you and you tease me about being a human sloth or a rubbish climber, that doesn't change the fact that we're brothers!'

Ted was silent. Was he going to hug Jonny? Smile? Thump him?

'Prove it,' said Ted. 'Before I come home, I need something more. I've been shut up for days in a warehouse that smells of fish, feeling miserable and rejected, and I need some proof. Prove, somehow, that you are properly sorry and actually deserve to call yourself my brother.'

'Actions speak louder than words, I find,' said Henry.

Ted jumped. 'Who said that?'

Henry juddered, as if ruffling invisible feathers, and became brilliantly visible to everyone. Ted, J2 and Pete-Pip gawped, speechless. Hari was too busy eating a beetle to care.

'It's just the ghost of Henry the Eighth,' said Jonny, as if it was totally normal to be hanging out with a dead Tudor monarch. 'And I *will* prove it.'

'Prove that he's Henry the Eighth?' said Ted. 'Seems pretty obvious, really. Check out those robes!'

'No!' said Jonny. 'Prove that I deserve to

be your brother. Prove I'm sorry. Prove I care.'

'How?' asked Ted.

Jonny thought for a second, then looked beyond Ted to a tree a little way off. On a high branch, blowing gently in the breeze, was a large pair of men's pants. They were slightly torn and a little dirty, but you could still clearly make out a pattern on them – cars.

'That's it!' said Jonny, pointing at the tree. 'I've got it! I'M GOING TO TOUCH THE HANGING PANTS OF DOOM!'

CHAPTER THIRTY-NINE

THE CLIMB OF HIS LIFE

Immediately, Jonny raced over to the tree and began to climb. The Hanging Pants of Doom were stuck on a high branch, much higher than Jonny had ever climbed before. Ted and J2 watched from their tree, Pete-Pip and Henry stared up from below and Hari just kept on eating beetles, as Jonny slowly but determinedly pulled himself up through the branches.

'I'm not sure this is a good idea, Jonny,' shouted Ted. 'You're not a great climber.'

'He is kind, though,' said Pete-Pip. 'I mean, you can say that for him, can't you?'

'Sorry, who are you?' Ted asked.

'I'm Pip, one of Jonny's Sibling Swap

brothers,' she said. 'He was good to me. He tried to get me off the Xbox in the middle of the night so I could rest. I was doing this whole "I'm addicted to Xbox!" acting thing to test out Sibling Swap and sort of force him to send me back, so I could see how it all works. I'm not even a boy, as you can see! Anyway, he was very patient with me, even when I was being pretty awful. He also wanted us to go for a walk so we could hang out together, which was nice.'

Hari squeaked in agreement, then went back to his beetles. Then Henry spoke.

'He showed that he was brave and loyal too,' said the dead king. 'He looked after your mother, who unfortunately fainted away when she saw me. (It happens.) He defended his dog and was determined to find you and establish the brother bond again. These are excellent characteristics. You're a fine fellow, Jonny.'

'You got my name right,' muttered Jonny, smiling briefly, before reaching for the next branch.

'He also saved Alfie's life,' Henry added.

'He did what? To who?' Ted gasped.

'Another brother – Alfie,' said Henry. 'A bit of a rogue. The little fellow climbed a tree

and then fell. Jonny saved him with a box of sweetmeats. I observed it all in my all-seeing ghostly way.'

'A box of … Oh, never mind,' said Ted. 'Is this true, Jonny? Did you save a boy's life?'

There was no answer, though. Over in his tree, Jonny was now up high. All the brothers stared up at him. He was clinging to a branch with one arm while the other arm was slowly, slowly, slowly reaching out towards the Hanging Pants of Doom.

CHAPTER FORTY

GRIPPING!

'STOP!' yelled Ted. He vaulted down to the ground and ran over to Jonny's tree. 'Jonny, stop! You've proved you are my true brother. You don't need to touch the pants for me! Please, come down.'

Jonny let out a sigh of relief and, still clinging to the branch, slowly looked down. He wanted to see Ted's face, capture this moment, share a smile, give his brother the thumbs up. But as he waved his upturned thumb he also noticed the ground far, far below. He had climbed higher than he'd ever climbed before, determined to prove to Ted that he was a worthy brother, but now the ground seemed to be rushing up towards him. He felt dizzy. His arm waved madly as he flailed, dipped,

263

tried to grab on to the branch again and, horror of horrors ... GRABBED THE HANGING PANTS OF DOOM INSTEAD!

A cry of **'NOOOO!'** went up from everyone below as Jonny grasped the pants. They came loose from the branch and hung limply in his fist. He stared at them, frozen, one hand wrapped tightly around a branch, one holding the dreaded, terrible underwear.

Would he scream? Fall? Throw up? All three at once?

Nope!

Instead, he laughed. A quiet laugh of surprise, which rippled into a full, throaty laugh of glee.

I've done it, he said to himself. *I've done the thing I was always so scared to do. And, actually, it's OK. The Pants of Doom are just old pants, with cars on. That's all. Ha!*

He gazed at them a little longer, then stuffed the pants into his pocket.

'Are you all right?' Ted shouted up at him.

'Yeah,' he said, as he began his slow, careful descent. 'Never better!'

Safely on the ground once more, Ted slapped Jonny on the back and grinned at him.

'You absolute nutter,' he said.

'Proved I'm your brother, though,' said Jonny.

'You definitely did,' said Ted. 'Now, can we please go home?'

'Yes!' said Jonny, and everyone cheered.

'Wait! No!' said Jonny. 'We have to set Alfie free and those other kids in the warehouse. But let's be quick. I still don't know who's behind Sibling Swap, but they won't be pleased if they catch us releasing their swaps.'

'Aren't you going to lob the Pants of Doom back up in the tree first?' asked Ted, but Jonny didn't hear him. He was already heading out of the copse, his band of brothers running along behind him.

CHAPTER FORTY-ONE

THE TRUTH IS OUT

Jonny stopped at the edge of the industrial estate, with the Sibling Swap warehouse a little way off. He turned to his brothers.

'The plan is to set Alfie and any other children free and then get out of there,' he said. 'Let's be quick. Pete-Pip, send the drone out and check the coast is clear around the warehouse.'

'On it,' said Pete-Pip.

'The rest of us need to find the keys and get those children out as fast as possible,' said Jonny.

'No sign of anyone in there,' said Pete-Pip, checking the drone footage on her small laptop. 'You're clear to go!'

Hari skittered back to his tunnel as the others ran silently towards the front door. Inside, Henry ghosted through walls, searching for the keys. He soon found them, hanging on a peg, hidden behind the freezers. He lobbed them to Ted, who began unlocking the cubicle doors and releasing the children inside. Alfie raced out of his cubicle and bounced all over Jonny. Then Jonny heard someone coming. Before he and Alfie could hide, the door swung open and in walked ...

'George!' shouted Jonny. 'What are *you* doing here?'

George looked a bit guilty. Then Jonny's eyes grew wider. The smell of fish fingers! The boxes full of dodgy gadgets! He'd been struggling to tie all these together, but now it all made sense. This was George's uncle's warehouse. But what was George doing here? Unless ... oh no, surely not ...

'Yes,' said George, 'Sibling Swap is mine. I, er, kind of created the website? With my techy skills, you know?'

'And don't tell me,' said Jonny, 'the whole dedicated team of Swap operatives who work day and night to find the right swap ...'

'You're looking at it,' said George. 'Just me, with my computer, in my bedroom.'

'You *idiot*!' said Ted, marching over and looking as red as furious ketchup. 'Your stupid website has caused so much trouble. It was a ridiculous idea!'

'Don't blame me!' yelled George. 'I haven't got a brother or sister, so how would I know? Anyway, it was Jonny who gave me the idea, always talking about how he'd had another fight with you and he wished he had a new brother.'

'That was just imagining and wishing,' said Jonny. 'I didn't expect anyone to let me do it. Anyway, I know now. You can't swap family members.'

'Yes, you can!' said George. 'I know some of your brothers haven't worked out, but it wasn't a total disaster, was it? I mean, at first, you seemed so excited about it.'

'At first, maybe!' Jonny spluttered. 'But, yes, it was a disaster. You can't just go around swapping brothers and sisters on the internet, with only a form to fill out. I've tried and it doesn't work. Plus, it's wrong. Really wrong. It's not, what's the word? Edible!'

'Ethical,' said Ted. 'It's not ethical.'

'Right!' said Jonny.

'I don't believe this!' shouted George. 'I did this for you, Jonny. I thought you'd be happy to be able to swap your brother. More children should have that chance! I know there must be hundreds of kids up and down the land who want to do it. I just need to sort out a few problems with the website, that's all. It's all on my laptop, here in my backpack. Just a few clicks and Sibling Swap will be unstoppable. I won't give up on it! This will change lives! I'll show you. I'll prove it!'

And with that, he ran out of the warehouse.

CHAPTER FORTY-TWO

DOWN TO THE RIVER

'Quick, after him!' yelled Jonny. He led the chase, with Ted running alongside. The other brothers followed, streaming behind in hot pursuit. George was running hard, a good way out in front, when suddenly he stopped. The river! He had run towards the river that flowed through the meadows on the edge of town, and now it was barring his way. The brothers soon caught up and formed a tight semicircle around him, with the rushing water at his back. He was trapped.

'Hand over that laptop,' Jonny said. 'Hand it over so we can put an end to all this swapping madness.'

'Never!' said George. 'Sibling Swap will

succeed! Children around the world will be grateful to me, an only child who solved the problem of siblings! Perfect!'

George suddenly turned and began climbing down the riverbank towards the water.

'What's he doing?' Jonny shrieked.

'He's got a boat, look!' shouted Ted. 'He's getting away! Stop him! *Stop him!*'

Too late! George had clambered into a tiny wooden boat, hidden in the rushes, and was drifting out into the middle of the river. He pulled his laptop out of his backpack and waved it at the brothers standing on the bank.

'Bye bye!' he called. 'Right here in this computer is the power to change lives. No one can stop me now! No one!'

No one? thought Jonny. *There must be someone who can help. Another brother ... Of course!*

'Mervyn!' Jonny gasped, and then he shouted, loud and clear, 'Mervyn, help! Mervyn! MERVYN!'

Silence. George floated further downstream, about to disappear round a bend in the river. The boys stood in silence. There was no Mervyn. George had got away. Jonny had failed. His shoulders sagged as he stared at the ground, miserable.

'What was that?' whispered Ted.

The boys all looked where he was pointing. There was a faint movement beneath the water, a flash of silver, a ripple.

George didn't see it. He was still waving the laptop at the boys and giving them a gloating thumbs up. He didn't notice the top half of a boy appear from the water behind his boat. He never spotted the triumphant flick of his gorgeous fishtail as he leaped into the air like a dolphin.

'Mervyn!' gasped Jonny.

'Wowwwwwww!' gasped all the other brothers as the boy flew up, grabbed the laptop and splashed back down beneath the surface, taking it to watery destruction.

'My laptop!' roared George, peering over the side of the boat. 'No!'

He began paddling his hands desperately in the water and then, leaning forward a touch too much, tumbled head first into the river. Quickly, Mervyn swished alongside, pulling the spluttering boy up and tossing him back into the boat.

'Perhaps you should stay there for now,' said Mervyn. 'I might not be around to save you next time.'

George sprawled, soaking and exhausted in the bottom of the boat, while Mervyn swam over to greet Jonny.

'You came!' said Jonny. 'You heard my call!'

'That's what brothers are for!' said Mervyn, and he splashed his tail vigorously, sending a shower of droplets over the boys, who all whooped and cheered and punched the air.

'Mervyn, you're the best!' shouted Jonny, above the sound of laughter and high-fiving. They had done it! The laptop was destroyed, the children were free, Ted was Jonny's brother again, it was all ...

BARK BARK!

The group froze, silent. It wasn't Hari this time. This was a deeper bark, an angrier bark.

BARK! BARK!

There it was again! The boys turned to see Fatso the guard dog running towards them, all teeth and slobber and fur. He had chewed through his rope and, furious at seeing all the children escaping, was bombing towards the boys at full speed. There was only one thing to do ...

'RUN!' yelled Jonny.

Instantly, the group scattered. Alfie scampered up a nearby willow tree and Hari disappeared down an old burrow in a very meerkatish way. J2 and Pete-Pip hid behind Henry and his giant robes, but the dog hardly noticed. He had someone else in his sights. Ted! He was tearing after Ted, chasing him into a patch of dense undergrowth. Ted jumped and swerved and ducked his way through, but

the dog was gaining on him. Suddenly, he came to a dead end, a thick hedge of brambles barring his way. He was stuck!

Fatso was crouching now, ready to pounce, teeth bared, a deep growl rumbling like thunder in his throat.

Ted was shaking, unable to get away. He shut his eyes, waiting for the animal to sink its teeth into him. All he could hear was growling, growling, growling, then **WHEEEEE!**

Ted's eyes pinged open.

Jonny had grabbed some yoghurts off Henry and was lobbing them at the dog.

'LEAVE! MY! BROTHER! ALONE!' roared Jonny, chucking another one, which exploded against a tree trunk like a milky firework. The dog instantly forgot about Ted and began licking the creamy splats instead.

'Quick, Ted, get over here while the dog's distracted,' shouted Jonny.

Ted dodged past the huge animal, still happily licking up yoghurt.

'You saved me!' he said.

'No problem! It's the least I can do for my brother!'

Then Jonny grinned at him and Ted opened his arms and folded his little brother into a warm hug. Jonny basked in that hug. It was a great hug. Probably one of the best hugs he'd ever had.

The warm feeling soon evaporated when Jonny opened his eyes. Looking over Ted's shoulder, he could see Fatso, who had finished the yoghurt and was now snarling at the two brothers.

'UH OH!' he said, shoving Ted towards the tree Alfie had climbed up as the dog began loping towards him, teeth bared.

'Go, Ted, go!' Jonny shrieked. 'Climb that tree!'

'You too, Jonny. Come on!' Ted screamed as he pulled himself up on to a branch. But Jonny didn't move. He held his ground. He had no more yoghurts, but his hand found something else in his pocket.

'Quickly, Jonny, climb up!' shouted Ted. But Jonny wouldn't budge. He stood firm, a small boy standing between his brother and a very angry dog. *Well, I never was much good at climbing*, Jonny thought, and then …

GRRRRR!

Fatso ran at him, and as the huge dog got closer Jonny gripped the soft-something in his pocket. A tissue? A baby squirrel? No, it was a large pair of men's pants. A large pair of men's pants with cars on. The Hanging Pants of Doom! Of course! But Jonny was no longer scared of them. He had conquered his fear the moment he pulled them out of that tree. They worked for *him* now!

As Fatso leaped towards him, front paws in the air, ready to flatten him, Jonny flung his secret underwear weapon. The pants flew out, opening up like a matador's cape and landing perfectly on the dog's face, covering his eyes and hooking around his ears. Now Fatso couldn't see, which was good, but he also couldn't stop. Which was less good.

WHAM!

The full force of a high-speed forty-kilogram guard dog, now wearing pants on his head, hit Jonny squarely in the chest. He was thrown to the ground. He felt a bright pop of pain and saw a flash of white light as his head cracked against the hard ground. Then he blacked out.

CHAPTER FORTY-THREE

ALL BETTER NOW

When Jonny woke up he was not at home. He was not by the river either. But, looking around the room, he realised with a huge wave of relief that he was not alone.

Ted stood next to his bed. A hospital bed. Jonny lifted his hand to his head and winced. He had cuts and grazes on his scalp and a black eye. They all hurt.

'About time you woke up!' said Ted. 'You've been out of it for ages. It's half past nine at night! Mum was here, but she's just gone to get a coffee.'

'What happened?' murmured Jonny.

'Saved by the pants!' said Ted. 'Once Fatso knocked you down, he forgot about killing you and went running about, shaking his head like mad, trying to get the pants off. He eventually fell straight into the river and got swept down to George, and clambered into his boat. Sadly, the pants got washed away. But hey, that was some smart pant-throwing, brother! Though I still can't believe you risked getting eaten by a dog to save me! You already proved you were a good brother by touching the Hanging Pants, anyway. You didn't have to go that far.'

'Actions speak louder than words,' said Jonny. 'King Henry taught me that!'

'Yes, I did,' said Henry, ghosting through the wall. 'I always knew you were a man of valour, Jonny!'

'Thanks, Your Specialness,' said Jonny. 'What happened to George?'

'That knave!' said Henry, narrowing his eyes. 'He deserves chastising roundly, but in fact, young Peter-Pipper has taken him under her wing.'

'Just to translate,' said Ted. 'Pete-Pip has decided to hold coding sessions in our shed with George, to keep an eye on him and also to help him channel his computer skills into something more sensible than a sibling-swapping website.'

'Great idea,' said Jonny.

'She's taken Sibling Swap down so there's no trace of it now *and* she's threatened to wipe all George's hard drives if he dares try anything like that again.'

'So all's well that ends well,' said Henry. 'Being your brother has been a glorious diversion, Jonny, just as I hoped, but I see I could never replace Ted. Alas, Sibling Swap does not work, it appears. I think we can all agree on that! I shall retire to the Other Side and let you be at peace.'

Then Henry wafted away like royal smoke.

'What happened to everyone else?' Jonny asked. 'Did Mervyn go back to the sea?'

Ted nodded. 'Sends his love,' he said. 'He's a bit too fishy for dry land. He did help himself to a few dodgy fish fingers before he went, though. Does that make him a cannibal?'

Jonny laughed and then winced. Ted put a hand on his brother's shoulder.

'Sorry you got beaten up by Fatso,' he said. 'I never wanted you to get hurt. Honest. Well, a bit. No! Not really! Joking!'

A grape bounced off Jonny's head.

He looked up to see Pete-Pip, J2, Alfie and Hari bounding into the room, all talking – or in Hari's case, squeaking – at once.

'OK, people,' Ted shouted above the racket. 'Don't crowd him out. He's been through a lot. And don't jump on his bed, Alfie! J2, stop lobbing grapes!'

'We're all going home!' Alfie shouted, jumping up and down on the floor. 'And Pete-Pip traced Hari's true parents. They're going to build a gigantic sandpit for him in their garden.'

Hari squeaked excitedly.

'And I've got my own brother back,' said J2, shoving a boy who looked rather like Ted through the crowd towards Jonny. 'Meet Fred. Turns out he had a rough time with Sibling Swap too. Got sent all kinds of funny matches. He's apologised for putting me on the site, just like you did to Ted, so we're all good.'

'Can we see you again?' Alfie asked. 'Once you're better? We might not be proper brothers, but we make an amazing team! I bet you say yes!'

Jonny just grinned at his new and unlikely band of almost-brothers.

'Better get going, guys,' Ted said. 'I'm his big brother and I say the patient needs to rest!'

'Quite right,' said a doctor, who had just arrived and was watching the boys. The brothers all promised to keep in touch, waved, grinned, squeaked, saluted, scoffed a few grapes, and then left.

Jonny waved and then winced again.

'That will be the broken ribs,' said the doctor.

'This is Doctor Jones,' said Ted.

'And this is my brother!' said Jonny, pointing at Ted. Crumbs, it felt good to say those words.

'I know,' said the doctor. 'He's been very worried about you, Jonny – hasn't left your bedside. You're lucky. Not all brothers get along so well. Have you always been close?'

Jonny and Ted burst out laughing, with Jonny wincing between giggles.

'Not always, no,' said Ted.

'He gives me lots of wedgies,' Jonny added.

'He tried to replace me with that bunch of new brothers he found on the internet,' said Ted.

'But I said I was sorry!' said Jonny. 'And I nearly got killed for you!'

'That was pretty stupid, though,' said Ted. 'You idiot!'

'Don't call me an idiot,' said Jonny.

'*Ahem!*' said the doctor. 'You will be able to continue this little discussion at home, but not yet. Jonny, you blacked out for a while, so I want to keep an eye on you a bit longer. Ted, you can take your brother home tomorrow. How does that sound?'

Ted looked at Jonny. For a terrifying second, Jonny wondered if he was going to say, 'No way! You must be joking! After everything he's done? Can't you keep him here?'

Then Ted grinned. 'That sounds great,' he said. 'Right, loser?'

Jonny nodded gratefully. 'Right!' he said. 'Home. With my brother. That sounds like the best idea I've heard in a really long time!'

HEAD TO
www.siblingswap.com
TODAY

... your future sibling awaits!

⋆ ⋆ ⋆

Change brothers and switch sisters!

Sometimes you don't get the brother or sister you deserve,
but here at Sibling Swap, we aim to put that right.
With so many brothers and sisters out there,
we can match you to the perfect one!

So what are you waiting for?
Get SWAPPING!

⋆ ⋆ ⋆

- Take the quiz to find your perfect brother or sister
- Meet the founder of Sibling Swap
- Download fun activities and games to play with
  (or without) your sibling!